The City That Care Forgot

Liliana Hart

A Letter From the Author

Dear Readers,

I'm excited to share with you that I've recently gotten the rights back to several of my earliest books. The Lies We Tell was actually the very first book I ever wrote, and it holds a special place in my heart. This book has been completely revamped and updated, with new scenes added. I'm so glad I get to share it with you again. Whether you've read the earlier version, or you're brand new to Gabe and Grace's story, I think you're going to love reading The Lies We Tell.

Happy Reading,
    Liliana

Also by Liliana Hart

JJ Graves Mystery Series

Dirty Little Secrets

A Dirty Shame

Dirty Rotten Scoundrel

Down and Dirty

Dirty Deeds

Dirty Laundry

Dirty Money

A Dirty Job

Dirty Devil

Playing Dirty

Dirty Martini

Dirty Dozen

Dirty Minds

Addison Holmes Mystery Series

Whiskey Rebellion

Whiskey Sour

Whiskey For Breakfast

Whiskey, You're The Devil

Whiskey on the Rocks

Whiskey Tango Foxtrot

Whiskey and Gunpowder

Whiskey Lullaby

The Scarlet Chronicles

Bouncing Betty

Hand Grenade Helen

Front Line Francis

The Harley and Davidson Mystery Series

The Farmer's Slaughter

A Tisket a Casket

I Saw Mommy Killing Santa Claus

Get Your Murder Running

Deceased and Desist

Malice in Wonderland

Tequila Mockingbird

Gone With the Sin

Grime and Punishment

Blazing Rattles

A Salt and Battery

Curl Up and Dye

First Comes Death Then Comes Marriage

Box Set 1

Box Set 2

Box Set 3

The Gravediggers

The Darkest Corner

Gone to Dust

Say No More

Copyright © 2023 by Liliana Hart
All rights reserved.

Published by 7th Press
Dallas, TX 75115

All rights reserved. This book or any portion thereof may not be reproduced or used in any manner whatsoever without the express written permission of the author except for the use of brief quotations in a book review.

This is a work of fiction. Names, characters, businesses, places, events and incidents are either the products of the author's imagination or used in a fictitious manner. Any resemblance to actual persons, living or dead, or actual events is purely coincidental.

"In other places culture comes down from on high. In New Orleans, it bubbles up from the streets."
—*Ellis Marsalis*

Chapter One

The *slap, slap, slap* of his shoes hitting the pavement echoed in the fog that crept over the sleeping city.

He was slicked with sweat and his lungs burned with each laboring breath, but still he ran faster, punishing his body, punishing himself, as he fought the urge to look over his shoulder. It never seemed to matter how fast he ran, because his past continued to haunt him.

Shane Quincy knew all about ghosts and personal demons. He knew about the terror of the innocent and their screams that still filled his head. He knew about heartbreak and sorrow because it plagued him with every breath he took. And most of all, he knew about fear—fear that clawed its way up from the pit of his belly and left a bitter taste in his mouth—and horrors so devastating they could break the soul of a man who'd been trained for the worst humanity had to offer.

He'd been the best the government had to offer. But even his best hadn't been good enough.

He slowed his steps as a heavy drizzle blanketed the deserted New Orleans street and hunched over, propping his hands on his knees as he gasped for breath and tried to ease the aching in his chest. He knew from experience that the ache would never go away, but he tried just the same.

For two years his routine hadn't changed. The nightmares would come, waking him in a cold sweat with the taste of bile rising in the back of his throat. The covers would be damp and twisted beneath his restless body and his senses would be primed. But the echoes of the screams were only in his imagination, so he'd slip on his sweatpants and a T-shirt, leave his empty apartment, careful not to disturb the dark-haired woman in 3A, and he'd run for miles through the Big Easy. Fast and hard, as if he were running for his life. And in some ways he was.

The drizzle turned into a downpour and Shane laughed bitterly as he raised his face to the sky. He began running again, this time at a slower tempo, and turned left off First Street onto Prytania.

The old white gothic mansion sat on the corner, surrounded by stooped oaks that dripped Spanish moss, and a black iron fence gave the residents a semblance of privacy. He never would have been able to afford the place when he was working for the FBI, but he'd found out very quickly that moving into the private sector offered him a way of life he'd never imagined. Of course, he'd never meant to live that life alone. But here he was.

His skin was chilled and his dark hair, which was in desperate need of a trim, dripped into his eyes as he typed in the security code for the wrought-iron gate that protected him and the other residents. Only four of the six units were occupied, the effects of the pandemic still making people wary of putting down roots.

There was a young couple on the first floor, both of them Loyola law graduates and college football fans based on the weekly gatherings they hosted. They'd given him an open invitation to stop by anytime, but being around people for long periods of time tended to make him itchy.

There was a tenured NOU professor who lived on the second floor. He tended to have frequent overnight houseguests, many of them young enough to be his grad students, and he liked to cook. Shane knew this firsthand because his balcony was just below his own and he often left the French doors open.

Then there was the woman who'd moved in across the hall from him a few weeks before.

She was quiet. He never heard her television or

radio on. She had Chinese food delivered at least once a week, and she didn't stick to any pattern of coming and going at particular times of the day. She hadn't had any visitors and she was skittish to the point that every time he passed her he felt like he needed to look over his shoulder, just to make sure.

Despite her neighborly qualifications, he found her presence irritating. It had been two years since the longing for a woman had reached up from inside him and taken hold. He'd not felt anything in the two years since Maggie had died. Nothing but emptiness and grief and anger.

But this woman had broken his fast. She was Maggie's complete opposite—hair dark as night and piercing blue eyes—and she walked with a confidence that would intimidate most men. Most being the key word. He'd never been like most men. And he'd always enjoyed a good challenge.

But every time he felt the attraction come over him, it was followed by a rush of shame. As if he were being disloyal to his wife. Parts of him had died with her, and dead men weren't supposed to feel things.

The gate clattered closed behind him, and he moved quickly to the side of the house where white wooden staircases led to the upper floor apartments. Shane was almost to the third floor before he smelled the smoke. The rain and the wind had dampened the scent so it was barely recognizable, but it was there. He was sure of it.

He raced the rest of the way up the stairs to the third floor and saw the licks of flame taunting him from the windows. The sight was hypnotic, the reds and oranges of the fire as it danced a path of destruction. The front door and one of the windows were open, feeding the inferno with much-needed oxygen so it spread quickly through the rooms, up the thick drapes and onto the ceiling. And even from the entrance he could smell the pungent scent of gasoline.

Black smoke billowed out the open window and door, and he cursed himself for leaving his cell phone on his nightstand. Fire alarms shrieked and he hoped the other tenants heard them.

He didn't pay attention to the splintered wood on the open door as he charged into the smoke and biting flames to see if his neighbor was still inside. His adrenaline was pumping and he didn't miss the irony of the situation, that a failure such as himself would be put in the role of hero once again. He hadn't been able to save anyone in a long time. He could barely save himself.

Their common entryway was filled with smoke and he kicked at her door, splintering the old wood. Her apartment was a mirror image of his own, and he ran sense instead of sight down the long hallway to the bedrooms at the back.

Paint blistered the walls. Black smoke blurred his vision and clogged his lungs, so he ducked down on his hands and knees and crawled the rest of the way to the bedroom. The fire wasn't contained to one area but seemed to be everywhere at once, racing toward some unseen finish line where the prize was utter destruction. The blaze was scorching hot and windows shattered as the pressure built hotter and higher inside the fiery walls.

Shane heard the coughs and the pants that sounded more animal than human as he crawled over the threshold into the master bedroom. The air was slightly clearer, but it wouldn't be for long. He stood up quickly and used his shirt to wipe his burning eyes before taking stock of the situation. What he saw built a fury in his gut that he hadn't felt in a long time.

The woman was handcuffed to the wooden slats on her headboard, her eyes wide and panic stricken, and they became even more so when she saw him enter the room. The lady was terrified, but not just of the fire. She was afraid of him, and her struggles became even more frantic. He knew she would have screamed if she could have, but the smoke was thick and she doubled over in a coughing fit. Her black hair was matted around her temples and the boxer shorts and tank top she'd been sleeping in were wilted and sweat slicked.

Her wrist was raw and bloody where she'd been pulling against her restraints.

"I'm not going to hurt you," Shane called out. He didn't know if she heard him or not, but he moved toward her anyway because they were running out of time. He could hear the blare of sirens from below, but it was up to him to get them both out alive.

He touched her on the shoulder and was caught off guard as she came up swinging with her free hand. It barely glanced off his shoulder, but he was impressed by her tenacity. She was no coward, that was for sure.

"I'm not going to let you kill me!" she screamed. "When I get out of here I'm going to send you back to my uncle in a body cast."

She fought against him like a caged animal until he wrapped both of his arms around her and squeezed tightly.

"I'm not going to hurt you," he repeated. "We've got to get out of here. We're running out of time."

She went into another fit of coughing and he used her distraction to kick at the wooden slats on the headboard. They were sturdy and thick, the antique obviously made to last centuries. Shane kicked again and put everything he had behind the force. The woman finally caught on that he was there to help and began pulling her weight against the steel bonds. A crack echoed through the room as the headboard gave way, and Shane barely caught her as the momentum from pulling against the cuffs almost sent them both to the floor.

Shane grabbed her around the waist and hauled her up over his shoulder. The smoke from the hallway was billowing into the room, so he carried her into the bathroom and shut the door behind him, buying them a few precious seconds. The large picture window behind the tub was the only way out. Black smoke crept under the door, and he grabbed one of the towels hanging on the hook next to the shower and shoved it beneath the crack in the door.

"Stand back," he said, grabbing the small vanity chair tucked under the counter and smashing it through the window. Fresh oxygen whooshed into the room and he gulped in a breath before the smoke found the opening he'd made.

Shane looked down three stories to the ground below. He'd been in a lot of deadly situations and thought he was going to die on more than one occasion, and his mind immediately started searching for ways to solve the problem. It wasn't over until it was over.

They couldn't jump three stories. It was out of the question.

The bathroom window overlooked the side of the house, and if he leaned out far enough he could see the wide wraparound porch that led to their front doors. Black smoke still billowed out the front door and open windows, but the fire department was at work, taming the beast as best they could with gallons of water. If he could throw her far enough and then jump himself, they might just have a chance. It was their only option.

Shane glanced at the woman and noticed her eyes were wide with shock. He stripped his shirt off and used it to clear the glass shards from the window so he didn't cut them both to pieces.

"How you doing, sugar?" he asked, swiping his thumb across her sooty face. "Don't go into shock on me yet. I'm going to toss you over to the railing. Do you think you're strong enough to grab hold?"

She nodded, but her eyes were glassy and he wasn't sure she really understood what he was about to do. "I'm strong enough," she assured him. "And I'm not your sugar."

Shane smiled, impressed with her bravado. Most women he knew would be in a heap at his feet. "Yes, ma'am." He grabbed her around the waist, lifting her, until he'd maneuvered them so he straddled the windowsill. "Use your feet to propel you," he instructed as he showed her where to place her feet.

"On three," he said.

He waited for her nod and began to count. "One, two..."

Shane heaved with all his might at the same time that she pushed off the windowsill. Time was suspended as she flew through the air. His heart thudded in his chest as he waited—what seemed an eternity but was only seconds—until she caught the railing with both hands.

He took a split second to heave a sigh of relief and then went after her, propelling himself off the ledge with a survival instinct that had been lying dormant for two years. He climbed over the railing quickly and helped pull her over before grabbing her around the waist and hurtling down the stairs as fast as his legs could carry them.

Shane noticed the other tenants standing back away from the house in their nightclothes. They were unharmed and stood transfixed as the wild orange fire was conquered. The cop in him looked around to see if anyone was overly interested in the blaze, but there was no one that stood out in the crowd. He noticed the woman was doing the same, but she was fading fast into exhaustion and shock. If someone wanted to kill her, she would be an easy target after the ordeal she'd just gone through.

The EMTs met them both with oxygen, and a cop unlocked the cuff around the woman's wrist. Shane could tell the officer wanted to ask questions, but the woman went into another fit of coughing and he backed off so the medics could do their job. Shane stayed as close to her as he dared and kept his eyes moving over the faces in the crowd. The lady had some explaining to do, and he wasn't going to let her out of his sight until she answered his questions.

The medics tended to her wrist, wrapping it in gauze and tape, and then left the two of them sitting in the back of an ambulance. Shane took the oxygen mask off his face and turned to look at her. She met his gaze with weariness and distrust.

"I'm Shane Quincy," he said, extending his hand. "I live across the hall from you."

"I bet between your looks and that accent there aren't many women who don't fall at your feet the second you open your mouth." She said the words through chattering teeth, which dulled the bite he was sure she intended, and looked at his hand like it was poisonous before briefly returning the handshake.

He arched a brow and smiled at her, enjoying the irritation that played across her face. "It was just an introduction, sugar. I don't expect women to fall at my feet until the second conversation. I'm a real gentleman like that."

"I didn't recognize you when you came in my room," she said. "I guess I should thank you for saving my life."

"I'd settle for your name." Shane could tell she was thinking about lying to him. "Your real name."

"Rachel."

"Do you have a last name, Rachel?"

"Just Rachel," she said firmly.

"Well, just Rachel, do you want to tell me who your uncle is and why he sent someone to murder you?"

Jimmy Grabbaldi knew his plan was going to fail as soon as he saw Rachel's neighbor appearing out of the misty rain like a phantom. Who the hell jogged in the middle of the night, anyway?

But he decided to stay and watch the scene play out. Maybe he'd end up with two casualties instead of one. As long as the job got done. That's what was important.

He'd done surveillance on the big white mansion for the last two weeks, snapping pictures of the tenants and their patterns as he made his way to the market or daily walks in the park across the street. There was a church on the opposite corner and an old graveyard that did daily ghost tours. There were plenty of secluded areas hidden by magnificent trees and large shrubs, and though the air was chilly once the sun went down, the weather was still warm and slightly humid in the daytime.

Jimmy couldn't have hidden his Italian roots if he wanted to. New Orleans was one of the most populous cities for Italian immigrants, and in general it was a melting pot for culture, so he embraced his heritage and didn't try to fit in with the tourists. He'd managed to secure an Airbnb in the Garden District and could see his mark from his balcony. No one bothered him, and it was easy enough to get a read on everyone who lived in the house.

Except for Rachel's third-floor neighbor, everyone in the building did the same things, day in and day out. They talked with the same people, left at the same time, came home from the same direction. *Boring.*

The third-floor neighbor was different though. His name wasn't listed on the mailbox like the other tenants, and his schedule was erratic. He always dressed in black and he looked like the kind of guy who didn't miss much. In fact, Jimmy was certain the guy had spotted him when he was out for one of his daily walks. The police presence in the park had picked up that afternoon, and Jimmy had gone back to his room, watching them through his binoculars.

But the time had come, and he'd felt it was time to make his move and get back to Chicago.

He'd passed the evening at Pat O'Brien's Bar down in the French Quarter, nursing a couple of glasses of Irish whiskey and charming a waitress named Candy. He'd charmed her into inviting him over to her place once her shift was over, and he left with a spring in his step and a song in his heart. Murder and sex all in the same night. What a way to say goodbye to the Big Easy.

Jimmy didn't consider himself an attractive man. He skimmed just under six feet and had the body of a brawler and the crooked nose to prove it was true. His hair was dark, his eyes black and his scarred complexion was covered with a short beard, but he never had trouble scoring with the ladies.

He liked to think he carried a certain... charisma. It's how he'd risen through the ranks of the Valentine organization so quickly. He was a loyal foot soldier, but there was an authority and danger about him that made people sit up and take notice. And it just so happened that authority and danger attracted a certain kind of woman.

He'd left Pat O'Brien's just after 3 a.m. with a soft buzz and Candy's address in his pocket. If he timed it right he'd get the job done and have time for a shower before taking his car to meet Candy at six.

He didn't have anything with him—no ID or wallet—just a money clip with a couple thousand in cash for business expenses. He took his time and walked almost three miles from the French Quarter to Prytania Street in the Garden District.

The rain was an added bonus. Cops rarely left

their warm, dry cars for a random stop or to ask questions of otherwise suspicious characters. Besides, he was hardly the only person out walking in the rain in the middle of the night in New Orleans. It was a city that never slept, even in the rain.

He'd parked his car on a crowded side street adjacent to Rachel's apartment so he could get away quickly if things went wrong, but things hardly ever went wrong when he set out to do a job.

He walked behind a couple who staggered their way down the broken sidewalk, laughing uproariously and stopping to lift their faces to the rain or kiss passionately. A horse and carriage clopped by beside him, a raucous group of six in the back who were headed to their next bar. And a single man, lit by a gas lantern under a balcony, wailed out notes of sorrow on a gold saxophone.

From time to time, a patrol car would pass by, but no one was looking too hard at anything. The couple in front of him were getting more passionate in their kisses, and he watched, annoyed, as they slipped into the park to finish the job. All he needed was them drawing attention before attention was due.

A Confederate statue stood sentry in the center of the park, surrounded by benches and mossy trees, and he slipped through the open iron gates and stood behind the stone pillar while he waited for the couple to be thoroughly distracted.

They'd found a bench partially hidden behind a tree, and it wasn't long before their moans echoed the low rumbles of thunder. He checked his watch and then moved toward the thick bushes, where he'd hidden the small box with all his supplies. It held everything he needed—a tin can of kerosene, matches, old rags he'd made from clothes he'd gotten from a thrift store, a penlight, a crowbar, and finally, the handcuffs.

Torch work was his specialty, and he could set a fire in his sleep. Not just any fire, but the kind of fire that looked like it was living and breathing, stretching the walls of its cage until it burst free. He set the kind of fires that were meant for total destruction. They didn't call him "Jimmy Inferno" for nothing. He wasn't trying to hide Rachel's murder in the fire. The fire was his weapon. The cops would never trace it back to him. He'd be back on a plane to Chicago as soon as he gave Candy a sweet goodbye and zipped up his pants.

And if the fire didn't hit the target...well, then, there were other ways. She could only run so far with only the clothes on her back.

Jimmy knew the code to the gate. None of the tenants except the guy on the third floor had bothered to cover the numbers when they entered. He heard the wailing sax in the distance. He carried the box and its contents up the three flights of stairs, sweating slightly and huffing a bit by the time he reached the top.

It was black as pitch, so he had to pick at the thick tape that held the box closed by feel. When the box finally opened, he dug around for the penlight and stuck it between his teeth before getting out the crowbar. The door was sturdy, but the locks were flimsy and it was just the break he needed. The door splintered open and he was inside in just a few seconds. He immediately began dousing the rags and laying them around the apartment to make a trail to the front door. He poured the rest of the gasoline on the rugs and curtains and dumped the cardboard box in the middle of the living room before heading back to the bedroom.

She was lying on her stomach. A long expanse of pale leg was visible from where he stood. She'd left the bathroom light on, so he put the penlight in his pocket and pulled out the cuffs. He could see the curtain of her dark hair as it framed her face, and her breathing was slow and easy. It was a shame the boss wanted to knock her off. A waste of a good woman in his opinion. But the boss had his reasons. Rachel Valentine was a threat.

The quiet click of the cuffs being fastened to her wrist and then to the headboard didn't wake her—the empty bottle of wine sitting next to a thick novel and a pair of reading glasses on the nightstand had been a twist of fate. Jimmy figured he'd let her sleep through her death. It was the least he could do for Dom's daughter. Kind of a last tribute.

He struck a match as he walked back out the door and dropped it onto the soaked rags. They didn't flare and spread as quickly as he would have liked, but it would get the job done. He left the door open and started back down the stairs, looking for any potential witnesses.

He saw the jogger after he closed the front door behind him, and he immediately took cover behind the garbage bins. The guy was huge, and he looked like he knew how to handle himself. The man was a little over six feet with the kind of muscle that reminded him of his favorite MMA fighter, and the way he moved was deliberate and disciplined. If this guy had been at Pat O'Brien's, Jimmy had no doubt who Candy would have given her address to. Danger reeked from every pore.

He guessed it wasn't really a surprise to see the man charge ahead into the smoke and flames and through Rachel's door. A dangerous hero was not what they needed for a job that should've been an easy in and out.

Jimmy snuck back across the street to the park and watched the action from a distance. And when Rachel and the guy both came out together, Jimmy knew he'd failed. The boss wasn't going to be happy with this latest setback. His orders had been to get rid of Rachel and get the hell out of New Orleans, and Angelo Valentine wasn't one to give second chances very often. Jimmy was dreading the phone call he was going to have to make.

On second thought, maybe he wouldn't place the call just yet. He could follow her and take care of the problem in the next couple of days. He'd be back in Chicago before the weekend.

Chapter Two

Shane waited patiently for Rachel's answer and knew from experience it wasn't going to be good.

She took off her own oxygen mask and said, "I don't know what you're talking about." She hopped down from the back of the ambulance and tossed off the thermal blanket the paramedics had wrapped around her.

"I can see the smoke has addled your brain," Shane said, irritated, tossing off his own blanket and hopping down to follow her. "Let me see if I can jog your memory, sugar. Someone broke into your apartment, cuffed you to the bed, doused everything in gasoline, and then set your place on fire. Maybe people do things different up north, but down here that's considered attempted murder."

"How'd you know I'm from up north?" she asked.

"It's what I do," he said patiently. "I know things about people. How they talk, how they walk, what hand they write or shoot with. I'm an observer of people. Call it a skill set."

Her glare could have cut glass, and she straightened her shoulders and started to walk away, but she changed her mind and came back as a police officer headed in her direction.

"Not a fan of the police?" he asked. "You're going to have to come up with something. There's going to be questions."

"Just leave me alone," she said, unable to hide the panic in her voice. "I've got to get out of here. Everything I owned was in that apartment, and now it's gone. I have nothing."

"Which is just part of the reason you're going to need my help, sugar."

"I don't want or need your help," she said. "I'm perfectly capable of taking care of myself. I've been doing it a long time."

"Obviously," he said. "You did a bang-up job at hiding from whoever is trying to kill you. You move to a new place, but you don't know how to hide. All you're doing is leading them on a chase. Why don't you tell me about your uncle?"

Her body jerked with surprise at his question. "Wha—what are you talking about? I don't have an uncle. I don't have any family."

"Lord, you're a bad liar. That's another one of my skill sets. I can spot a lie a mile away. Though you're so bad at it I suggest never going down that path. So let's try again. When you first saw me come into your room you said very clearly that your uncle was trying to kill you. Moments of life and death are the times we're most honest with ourselves and other people. So one more time...why don't you tell me about your uncle. The cop that's headed your way is going to want some answers, and I could make things pretty difficult for you. He's going to want to know who did this."

Anger brought color into her cheeks and her eyes darkened. "The more people involved the worse this will get. I don't want anyone else to get hurt. It's not law enforcement's problem," she said, licking her lips nervously. "Or yours." She moved closer to his side when the cop approached. "I just want to get away from here."

Shane wanted to smile. He guessed he was the lesser of two evils. He'd already saved her life once, and she couldn't trust anyone else.

"That's an unusual request for New Orleans," he said. "Most people never want to leave the Crescent City. It's the birthplace of jazz. The Big Easy. The City that Care Forgot."

"What are you? A travel agent?" she asked, rolling her eyes.

"Just trying to get you to stop shaking long enough to talk to this nice officer," he said. "Looks like I'll have to try another tactic." He put his arm around her and pulled her into his heat. Her body shivered uncontrollably from the adrenaline overload and the cold night air.

"And to think I just thought you were a rude and surly neighbor," she said.

"I am," he assured her. "But it's too hard to take the New Orleans out of the man, and we're generally well-mannered and polite here. Southern hospitality at its finest."

Shane didn't recognize the cop who approached. His business and expertise put him in a position to know most of the top law enforcement officials in the city. If he didn't know them then they sure as hell knew him by reputation.

The cop nodded at both of them as he approached. "My name is Officer Broussard and I need to ask you a few questions about the incident tonight." His uniform was pressed and starched severely so raindrops slid off the fabric in big fat drops. The stiffness could be nothing but uncomfortable against his considerable bulk. The night air was cool, and the stinging rain made it even colder. Shane was only wearing his sweatpants and running shoes and Rachel the thin cotton boxers and T-shirt she'd slept in. She didn't even have shoes.

Shane pulled her even closer and she burrowed into his warmth. It had been a long time since he'd had that kind of human connection, and he was surprised the rain didn't sizzle off his sensitized skin.

Shane made a decision, and he squeezed Rachel's arm lightly as a signal, hoping she would follow along.

"Officer Broussard," he said. "It's been a rough night." An uncontrollable shiver wracked Rachel's body, and Shane was pretty sure she wasn't that good of an actress. At least he hoped she wasn't. The shiver did the trick though because Broussard's eyes softened and he looked at her with pity. "All she has left are the clothes she's wearing. She doesn't even have shoes. Is there any way we can come into the station tomorrow to answer your questions?"

Officer Broussard looked both of them over and then made his decision. "First thing in the morning," he agreed. "This was no accident, and the longer we wait the less likely we are to catch whoever did this. You're very lucky to be alive the way that fire spread."

"Fortunately, I have kind neighbors," she said.

He nodded and said, "Be careful," and headed to his cruiser.

"Listen," Rachel said, pulling away from him. "I really appreciate your help. I wouldn't be here if it wasn't for you, but you don't understand what you're dealing with. I have to get out of here, and I have to do it alone. They'll kill you too if you're with me."

Shane was glad she was finally starting to give him a little honesty. "I don't think you know who you're dealing with, sugar. But this isn't just about you anymore. Whoever did this could have killed everyone in the building tonight. Me included. I can take care of myself, and I can track down who's responsible a hell of a lot faster than Officer Friendly over there."

She was shaking her head and looked ready to run as far away from him and New Orleans as possible. "I can't ask you to do that," she pleaded.

"You don't have to. Besides, this is our very first date. It'll be a hell of a story to tell our grandkids. I'm not quite ready to let you get away now that I've met you and put a name to that stunning face."

"You're out of your mind. Leave it to me to move in next door to a complete lunatic."

Shane didn't acknowledge her statement. Maybe he was out of his mind. He wasn't one to act on impulse. Not ever. He'd been trained to think out scenarios for every situation. He didn't even know what this situation was yet, but it didn't matter because his priority had become keeping Rachel alive.

"Let's get out of here," he said, taking her by the arm and leading her over to a large black Tahoe. "I've got some things to pick up at my office."

"I don't even know you," she protested.

"That's all right, sugar. I have a feeling we're going to get to know each other real well before this is over."

He put his Tahoe in reverse, speeding away from the flashing lights and the dwindling crowd toward the Central Business District. Neither of them noticed Jimmy Grabbaldi watching from his hiding place across the street.

Commuter traffic was just getting started as they made their way down the rain-slicked streets toward Shane's office. There was still another hour of dark, and the rain had turned back into a miserable drizzle.

"What is it exactly that you do?" Rachel finally asked after several minutes of uncomfortable silence. She'd spent the short car trip with her arms folded across her chest and her eyes staring straight ahead, but she was all too aware of the man sitting beside her.

"I work in private security," he finally answered.

"Is that like a private detective?"

"It's whatever the client wants. Sometimes it involves bodyguard work, and sometimes it involves tracking down people who don't want to be found."

"How long have you been doing it?"

"What is this, a job interview?" Shane asked. "I told you I was qualified to help you with whatever your problems are. I can probably even dig up a few references if it makes you feel better."

The "mind your own business" signal couldn't have been stronger if he'd been wearing a sign, but Rachel had never been one to give up easily. If she had, she'd already be dead.

"I have a right to know who you are. You've shanghaied my life and not given me any choice in the matter. Of course, I can always walk away just as soon as you stop the car. No harm, no foul."

The threat was made, but Rachel didn't want to walk away. She was tired of running, tired of hiding, and tired of looking over her shoulder every time she went to the grocery store. She needed help. And fate had stepped in and given her a bodyguard for a neighbor.

"You look like a cop. But more," she said, eyeing him carefully now. She'd gotten plenty of looks at him in the two months she'd lived in New Orleans. She'd have to be dead not to notice the dark-eyed god who lived across the hall. He looked like a fallen angel. His hair was dark and longer than she usually preferred on a man, hanging just past his ears and over his collar. His skin was swarthy, and his eyes were so black that the pupil and iris couldn't be differentiated. She'd lie awake at night and listen to him run his fingers over the piano in his apartment, playing bluesy numbers, and imagine what those same fingers would feel like touching her.

He let out a soft breath and said, "I was a Marine sniper and did a couple of tours of duty, and then I did more of the same for the FBI Hostage and Rescue Unit."

Rachel flushed because she'd been staring at him so intently she'd forgotten what question she'd asked. Now was definitely not the time to be having inappropriate thoughts about a man she didn't even know. She looked at the hard set of his jaw and the white-knuckled grip he had on the steering wheel and knew it had cost him a lot to tell her that much about himself. She decided not to press the issue for now.

They turned on Tchoupitoulas Street and parked in front of a nondescript, beige, two-story building smashed between more of the same on either side. All the buildings had red awnings that hung over the sidewalk. Discreet gold letters painted on the window said, *Quincy Security and Investigations.*

"This is a lot bigger than I thought it would be," Rachel said.

"What, you were expecting some hole in the wall in the slums?"

"No, not exactly." But she hadn't thought it would be an operation as large as this. Shane Quincy must be very good at his job.

"I've got twelve men and women on staff full time. All of them are retired law enforcement of some kind."

Rachel let him usher her into a small waiting area where a receptionist's desk and large fish tank sat among cool shades of gray and blue. She watched as he locked the door behind them and headed up carpeted stairs.

"I've got a small apartment up here that I use when I'm working late. It's got some extra clothes. Unfortunately, I don't think my shoes are going to fit you."

"That's okay. I don't think your clothes are going to fit me either."

He laughed and the sound sent tingles down her spine. This was a dangerous man. He threw her a pair of dark gray sweats and white athletic socks and pointed her to a small bathroom.

"Go get dressed and then you need to start talking," he ordered. "I need to know what we're up against."

Rachel did as she was told without argument

because he'd said the magic word. We. She no longer had to face her fears alone. And maybe by the time it was all over, her father could finally rest in peace.

Shane took off his sopping clothes and threw them in a basket by the bathroom door. He pulled on worn jeans, a white shirt, and a flannel, and he exchanged his wet Nikes for a pair of dry ones.

He went over to the window and pulled down a slat on the blinds, peering out into the street below. It was just after six in the morning and the traffic was light. There wouldn't be anyone in the office for another couple of hours, but he planned to be long gone by then.

He sent his secretary an email letting her know he'd be out of the office for a few days on a case and to turn over any pressing matters to his second-in-command. Then he went to his safe and pulled out a stack of extra cash, two Glock .9mms, and a snub-nosed revolver to go in his ankle holster. He had plenty of ammunition. He put all of it into a black bag and went to a locked cabinet behind his desk. No matter how many handguns he owned, his true love was still a rifle.

He unlocked the cabinet and had just pulled out the M40 when he heard movement behind him. Rachel was silhouetted in the door, a halo of light shining behind her, with his sweatpants rolled up at the bottom and the sweatshirt hanging down to her knees.

His eyes roamed over her lazily, taking in her flushed cheeks and damp hair, and his body did a slow meltdown. He put the M40 down carefully on his desk.

"I need to leave the area as soon as possible," she said. "And there's still time for you to change your mind. You'll become a target. Everyone and everything you care about will become a target."

"I've been a target before," he said. "In fact, there are certain countries there is still a hefty price on my head. This is the life I live. You're not deterring me."

She nodded and said, "My name is Rachel Valentine."

Shane knew the name was familiar, but he couldn't remember why.

"My father was Dominic Valentine."

His eyes grew big at that bit of information and he muttered a short expletive.

"I see you've heard of him," she said with a forced laugh.

If she knew how well he'd known the Valentine brothers she would have run screaming for the door. Shane had spent so much time trying to ignore her since she moved in that he hadn't studied her features as carefully as he otherwise might have. But he recognized Rachel for who she was now. She'd only been about twenty the last time he'd seen her—her hair had been lighter, streaked with blond as if she'd just spent a few weeks on a tropical island somewhere. He'd been a rookie at the FBI then, and his first assignment had been the infamous mob family. It would probably be best if Rachel never knew how close Shane had come to killing her father.

He watched as she closed her eyes and tried to gather her composure. The woman was in big, big trouble. Dominic Valentine had been the head of the largest crime family still operating in the United States. They were based in Chicago, and Shane remembered reading that "Dom" as he was called by everyone, had gone missing just before he was supposed to testify in federal court.

"Why don't we sit down," Shane said, taking Rachel by the elbow and leading her over to a small love seat. "Take your time. Do you need some water?"

She hiccupped out a small laugh and shook her head. "No, I'm fine. I'm tougher than I look."

He imagined she'd have to be to grow up in the Valentine family.

"I'm going to give you the short version, because I really need to get out of here. I feel like I've got a target on my forehead, and the itch at the back of my neck has been getting worse since we left the house."

"Just give me enough to know what I'm dealing with," Shane said.

"My father was ready to get out of the business. He hadn't been the same since my mother was killed several years ago, and things got worse after my younger sister was killed last year."

Shane remembered reading those bits of information in the newspaper and thinking that crime, most definitely, did not pay. Both of the Valentine women had been taken out with very sophisticated car bombs.

"I'm sorry," he told her softly.

"He made the decision because of me. Because I was all he had left," she said. "I know in my brain that my father was a criminal. He did bad things. Things that I will never be able to justify. But he was a good father, and for that he deserves my love and devotion as a daughter."

"Nobody could fault you for loving your father," Shane said.

"No, but I'm what you might think of as collateral damage. When I say my father wanted out of the business to keep me safe, I mean that he wanted all the way out. And if he had to do time in federal prison because of his crimes he said it was worth it to keep me alive.

"He met with an agent named Donald Culver

and agreed to confess to all of his financial transgressions and compile a list of all active Mafia and their crimes if he and I could both be put in Witness Protection. You should have seen his face when he told me he was finished. He was so relieved. I didn't realize how old he'd gotten until that moment."

Shane let out a low whistle between his teeth. "That would be one hell of a list for someone who's been around as long as Dom."

"Yes, but after dad met with Agent Culver at the Federal Building in Chicago and turned over the list, he went missing."

"When was the last time you spoke with him?"

"We spoke on the phone just after noon on the day he disappeared. He was scheduled to appear at the courthouse for a deposition and to meet with the district attorney. He knew they were going to arrest him, but he didn't seem to care."

"What happened to the list after your father disappeared?"

"Agent Culver was found with his throat slashed floating in Lake Michigan. The list hasn't been seen since, and no other agents will even admit to having seen it."

"They'd be signing their death warrants." Shane thought about everything Rachel had told him so far, processing bits of information, storing and discarding as needed. "So why are they after you, Rachel?" Shane finally asked, coming around to the one thing that didn't make sense.

"Because my father made a mistake."

"What mistake?"

"My father was blind when it came to his brother. He believed all families should be loyal to each other, no matter the circumstance, but Uncle Angelo was never loyal to anyone but himself. Dad asked Angelo to protect me if anything should happen to him, and Angelo played him until he got the information he wanted.

"What information?"

"Dad told Uncle Angelo that he'd sent me a copy of the list for safekeeping."

Shane shook his head in disbelief. "You have the copy of the list?" he asked incredulously. The fact that Rachel was still alive was a testament to her own abilities.

Stark pain came into Rachel's eyes. "Yes. It's in a safety-deposit box in Chicago. This is the reason I know Angelo killed my father. Because if Dad were still alive I would have heard from him by now. Angelo wants the list, and he'll do everything he can to get it in his hands. I'm running out of places to hide where his men can't find me."

Shane thought of the tangles this particular situation would bring them. The worst-case scenario was that Angelo would torture them both before disposing of their bodies. The Valentine organization ran far and wide, and there would be few people along the way who could be trusted to keep them safe.

"So what do you say, Mr. Private Investigator? Am I too dangerous for you?"

Chapter Three

"I guess it's lucky for you I like dangerous women," Shane said after a minute of stunned silence. "We need to get out of here. You can tell me the rest on the way. You must be one hell of an amazing woman to have dodged them for this long."

"You don't grow up in the Valentine household without learning a few helpful tips, but I've felt Angelo's men breathing down my neck over the last couple of months."

Shane zipped up the black bag with the weapons, money, and a few other necessities and slung it over his shoulder. He turned off the lights so only the glow from the computer screen was visible. He grabbed Rachel by the hand and pulled her toward him. She barely came up to his shoulder in her socked feet.

"I have to say I'm not terribly sorry for meeting

you under circumstances such as these. And I'm not sorry for this either."

He put his hand on the back of her neck and brought her closer. Her eyes fluttered closed as his lips hovered a breath away from hers. He recognized the low pull in his gut as her body fit against him. He was prepared to explore—her taste and texture—prepared to savor the soft sighs that would follow. But as he brushed his lips gently against hers, he realized he'd made a mistake. He wasn't prepared at all. Her mouth was a banquet, her lips sweet and her sighs intoxicating. He could lose himself in her taste alone.

He pulled away, knowing that if he kissed her again there would be no turning back. The part of himself he'd kept rigidly locked away would take over all rational thought, and it could only end in pain for them both because he would never be capable of giving what a woman like Rachel Valentine deserved.

But Rachel surprised him when she wouldn't let him back away. She wrapped her hands around the back of his neck and pulled him closer.

"Mmm, again," she moaned.

He knew it was a bad idea, but his brain was being overruled by more basic needs. He captured her mouth in a scorching kiss that held two years of pent-up desire and longing. It was a kiss meant to stir passions, a kiss meant to threaten his control. It was carnal in its intensity as lips and tongues clashed.

He hadn't realized he'd been starved for the taste of a woman. But not just any woman. Only this one. What was wrong with him? He had to get a grip, and fast.

No sooner had the thought entered his mind than the windows facing the street exploded and a boom echoed where only seconds before the room had been filled with sounds of passion. Terror and adrenaline replaced the feeling in an instant, and Shane rolled and tucked Rachel beneath him. The rapid-fire sounds of bullets hitting the building continued as they belly crawled to the stairwell.

"Sounds like he's got an HK MP5," Shane said, his voice calm and low.

"What's that?"

"Submachine gun. He'll have to stop and reload in a minute. When he does we need to get to the back door. There's an alleyway behind us."

"Gotcha," she said.

He admired the fact she hadn't lost control at the first sound of gunfire. They hunkered down again as the shots continued. The bottom windows were being taken care of now.

"I never realized I had so many windows," Shane said. "My secretary is going to be pissed."

"Do you think he followed us when we left the

apartments?" Rachel asked. "I looked around, but I didn't see anyone who looked suspicious."

"Yeah, I did too, but there was plenty of cover to be found in the park across the street."

The gunfire stopped as suddenly as it had started and the silence left in its wake pulsed along with the pounding beats of their hearts.

"Let's go," Shane said. He grabbed the black bag and shoved Rachel in front of him, shielding her body with his own as he pushed her down the stairs and led her through a long corridor of offices to an oversized steel door. The door opened soundlessly on well-oiled hinges, and cold rain beat against their skin as they ran into a dark alleyway.

"What are we going to do?" Rachel asked.

"We've got to find an alternate mode of transportation. There's no way we can make it to the Tahoe without him seeing us." Shane looked around the alley and noticed an older model Toyota. The paint had peeled in several places, the fender was rusted, and the tires were bald. He didn't think the car would get them down the street, much less to Chicago.

"What about that?" Rachel asked, pointing to a black-and-chrome Harley parked a ways down the alley behind the corner bakery.

"My kind of woman," Shane said with a quick smile as he grabbed her hand and ran the rest of the way down the alley. He could only pray that the guy shooting out front wasn't smart enough to think about checking the back entrances, but chances were if this guy worked for the Valentine family then he was plenty smart.

Rachel straddled the bike behind him and her arms wrapped loosely around his waist. Seconds ticked away in his head as he touched wires together and heard the sweet purr of the engine as it started and echoed through the quiet. They wouldn't be able to keep the bike for long before it was reported stolen. It belonged to the tattooed bakery owner, and he'd notice it was missing as soon as he brought the first load of morning trash to the dumpsters.

"Do you know how to fire a gun?" Shane asked, giving Rachel a quick look over his shoulder as he held out the Glock.

"Point and shoot, right?" she answered with a smile that Shane couldn't interpret the meaning of.

"Just do the best you can." He revved the engine and shot out of the alley at a high rate of speed, studying every spot on the street he would have used to hide if he was the one doing the shooting. He caught the reflection of steel as the streetlight glanced off a weapon pointed in their direction.

"Nine o'clock," he yelled to Rachel as shots rang out and pinged into a car barely a foot from his front tire. The streets were slick with rain, but his mind and hands stayed in control as he guided the bike across the pavement. He didn't even flinch as Rachel fired three rounds in close succession. All three hit the corner of the building their attacker was shooting from. It was a hell of a shot, no matter how you looked at it, and it reminded him he knew absolutely nothing about Rachel Valentine other than the fact she sent his body into overdrive and came from a dangerous family who'd obviously taught her how to shoot to kill.

Rachel held on for dear life as Shane tore out of New Orleans like a bat out of hell. The feel of freedom washed over her with every mile that separated her from her hunter and giddiness and adrenaline was its own euphoria.

It was just past sunrise when they stopped in a small town outside of the city. Houses were few and far between and trees were thick and covered with vines. The fishermen and trappers who worked the bayous were long since gone and others were still fast asleep.

"What are we doing here?" Rachel asked. "Do you think we should stop so soon?"

"We've got to change vehicles. I guarantee the bike has already been reported stolen. It's only a matter of time before we're spotted."

Shane gave her a funny look and she wondered if she had bugs in her teeth from the motorcycle ride.

"Where the hell'd you learn to shoot like that?"

"At my daddy's knee, of course," she answered with an attempt at the thick Cajun accent she'd heard so many people speak with since she'd been in Louisiana. "I shot for sport in college. Team captain."

"If you ever want a job, lady, give me a call. You're almost as good as I am."

"I'd be glad to accept a challenge. Anytime. Anywhere." Rachel couldn't believe how brazen she was being with someone she barely knew. She'd never been much of a flirt, and she'd never been promiscuous, but there was something about Shane Quincy that made her want to throw up her hands and say, "To hell with it." Despite her father's notoriety, she'd lived a pretty sheltered life. Boyfriends had been few and screened carefully. Her roommate from college had been handpicked, and every tenant in her apartment building had had a thorough background check.

"Be careful. I never back away from a challenge," he said softly.

The intensity and heat in his stare was enough to bring a blush to her cheeks, and she looked everywhere but at him with a newfound purpose. "It doesn't look like we have a lot to choose from."

"We don't need anything fancy," he said. "Just something that will get us part of the way to Chicago."

Rachel watched as Shane looked in the windows of a beat-up pickup truck. It was parked at the mouth of the bayou next to an old wooden dock. "We don't need to go to Chicago. We need to go to Dallas."

"Wait. Rewind," Shane said as he looked up from his task of hot-wiring the truck. "Why do we need to go to Dallas? I thought the list was in a safety-deposit box in Chicago."

The truck started with a sputtering cough and Shane threw in his duffle bag and practically tossed her into the cab.

"Why are we taking this? It won't do us any good if we break down on the side of the highway."

"Listen to the purr of that engine, sugar. People down here drive older cars but they keep them in top shape. It wouldn't do them any good to try and evacuate for a hurricane and not be able to get their cars started. And we're taking this particular truck because the owner is obviously busy checking his traps for the day. Trappers don't usually come in until the afternoon, so it should give us plenty of time to get a head start."

"Oh," Rachel said.

"Now tell me why we're going to Dallas when the copy of the list is in Chicago."

Rachel bristled a little at the demand, but kept her mouth shut. She'd never been one for taking orders. "I work at a large interior design firm in Chicago. Worked," she clarified. It had broken her heart to give up the job she'd fought so hard for. Sacrificed for. "Dad called me on my cell at the office that last day. I was busy with client meetings, so I didn't give him as much time as I should have. As I wish now I had. He was excited and told me everything was going to work out just fine, and that Uncle Angelo would take care of me if anything went wrong. Dad was scheduled to meet with Agent Culver like I told you, and then give his deposition. I wished him luck, told him I loved him and hung up. I didn't give it another thought until I was told he was missing."

Rachel's voice cracked on a sob, but she pulled herself together. She hated to show any weakness. Especially in front of a stranger. Valentines did not cry. Her father always told her their enemies would constantly look for vulnerabilities, chinks in their armor. So she'd stood dry eyed next to her father at the funerals of her mother and sister, though she'd been dying on the inside. If she could hold it together then, she could sure as hell hold it together in front of Shane Quincy.

Rachel took a few minutes to gather her composure and was thankful Shane stayed silent. The rain had picked up and was coming down in blinding sheets, but Shane handled the truck smoothly, focused on the road ahead. She hadn't seen him lose that focus in any of the situations that had been thrown at them so far.

She spoke softer as she continued. "Just as I was packing my things away for the day a FedEx package landed on my desk. Someone at the front desk had signed for it and sent it up. Since it was sent to me at work I figured it was work related and shoved it into my briefcase. I didn't give it another thought until I unlocked the front door of my apartment."

"Let me guess," Shane said. "Someone had searched your apartment."

"Searched is too kind a word for what they did. They violated every inch of every space. Drawers were upended and furniture had been slashed to ribbons. My desktop was smashed to pieces on the floor and my laptop was gone. I took one look at the mess, turned around and got out of there."

"You're lucky you didn't run into the person responsible."

"Believe me, I know. I found out later that night on the news that my doorman's body had been found in the alley with multiple gunshot wounds."

"What did you do?"

"I took a taxi to the South Side and stayed in a dirt-cheap motel until the next morning. I didn't sleep a wink that night and jumped at every sound. When I opened the package that had been sent to me, I knew I held the power to destroy a lot of people's lives. I think my father knew he probably wouldn't live to see all the wrongs made right, so it's up to me now."

"That's a lot of pressure to put on someone you love," Shane said skeptically.

"My father was a good man," Rachel insisted vehemently. "He'd want me to do the right thing."

"So why are you in Louisiana instead of testifying before a grand jury, and how do you know that your father told Angelo he gave you a copy of the list?"

This guy was a hard nut to crack. It was a good thing Rachel wasn't looking for sympathy, because she felt sure he didn't possess the emotion. Her voice frosted over and was hard as ice when she continued.

"Because the police discovered a message when they found my doorman's body in the alley. Angelo's men had carved a warning into the poor man's chest, demanding that I turn over the list or I'd be next. A news camera got it on film, and I saw the whole thing with the rest of the world on the ten o'clock news. The next morning I borrowed a car from the lot of the motel I was staying at and drove back to Chicago."

"When you say borrowed, I take it you mean stole."

"Are you going to let me finish the story or not?"

"By all means," he said.

"I was at my bank just as they were opening, and I told the clerk I needed to put some things in my safety-deposit box. My father made sure I was prepared in case something like this happened, so I removed a duffle bag from the box similar to the one you carry. It was full of cash and IDs, an extra set of clothes and a couple of wigs. I made a copy of the papers and put the originals in the safety-deposit box. I changed clothes and hair in the restroom and walked out the front door without anyone noticing."

"I can put two and two together and assume you sent the copies of the papers you made to someone in Dallas. But that still doesn't answer my question. How are you supposed to turn this evidence over to the FBI if you're running away?"

Rachel looked at Shane and wondered not for the first time if she was getting more with him than she'd bargained for. She was out of people she could trust. The list had been short to begin with, but now most of them were dead, and she didn't want to involve her two closest friends in anything that could get them hurt. Trusting a stranger might be her best shot at survival. Or Shane Quincy could be working for her Uncle Angelo and kill her for the large price that had been put on her head. Her instincts were failing her, and for the first time she wondered if she could even trust herself.

Shane noticed the sudden fear in her eyes but stayed silent, quietly driving the stolen truck along rutted and muddy paths. They'd be in Texas before they hit a highway that wouldn't jar teeth or spew mud onto passing cars.

"You're not going to get rid of me so easy now," Shane said. "Whoever's after you could have burned down my house and they destroyed my business. I'm in this for the long haul, so you might as well stay on for the ride."

The quick show of fear she'd displayed disappeared. Shane felt her cool stare and the calculating gaze of her weighing the odds of putting her safety in his hands. He kept his grip relaxed over the steering wheel and waited for her to make up her mind.

"Fine, but I prefer to treat this as a business relationship."

His curse was short and obscene, but she wasn't rattled.

"Hear me out," she said. "I don't like being out of control, and I've never had much faith in my fellow man. In my world people don't just do things for others out of the goodness of their hearts. But money, honor and pride are always important. Especially in my family. So it makes sense to hire you and your agency to track down the list and protect me when I hand it over to the FBI. There's no reason I'd have to testify. I have no knowledge of any business dealings my father had going and don't care to. We'd have a binding contract until I feel I'm in no further danger. And if you do happen to be working for my Uncle Angelo, just know that what I plan to pay you for your services will be far more than anything he could ever dream to offer you. Uncle Angelo doesn't hold the strings to the Valentine bank accounts since my father's disappearance. I do."

Shane clenched his jaw and the throbbing pulse in his neck told him just how pissed off her proposal made him. He'd been through horrors she could never dream of, serving and protecting his country while watching his friends die. Did she think he knew nothing of honor? Of pride? But then he closed himself off to his anger and analyzed the real reason for being so upset, just as he'd been taught to do in the Marines. Yes, he was offended that Rachel didn't trust him more, but he could hardly blame her for that when he hadn't trusted anyone but himself in the last two years.

The problem was that he wanted her. All of

her. He wanted to know everything about her. What made her tick and what made her laugh. And how her body would feel wrapped around his in the middle of the night. And if she paid him for his services, then his pride and honor would be at stake. Two things he'd never been able to compromise. Which meant that Rachel Valentine was off limits.

"Fine," he agreed. "But you'll have to be satisfied with a verbal agreement. Organization at my office is a little spotty right now."

Chapter Four

Rachel breathed easier for the rest of the trip to Dallas. She'd found comfort in Shane's anger. She needed a clear head now more than ever, and keeping Shane Quincy and his scorching kisses at arm's length was exactly what she needed to get through this ordeal with a clear head and an unbroken heart.

The rain had disappeared as soon as they'd crossed the border into Texas, and the sun was shining brightly despite the briskness in the air. They'd stopped at Walmart just before lunch, and Shane had run in and grabbed her some clothes and a pair of shoes. She'd changed in the cab of the truck while Shane had switched license plates with the car next to them.

"So where are we going to get the list?" he

finally asked. "Did you send it to a friend down here?"

"No, I sent it to a lawyer who tried to prosecute Dad several years ago. I figured it would be safe in his hands. He's stuck with client privilege since I pay him a retainer. I think it would be best for both of us if we could get the list without having to go to Chicago. Angelo has eyes and ears everywhere, and they'll know the moment I step foot into the city."

Shane knew she spoke the truth. The farther they could stay from Chicago, the safer they'd be. "It was a smart plan. Very smart," Shane acknowledged. "I've got a couple of pay-as-you-go cell phones in the bag. Grab one and give the man a call. Let him know we're coming to see him."

Rachel's own cell phone was still back in her apartment, so she had to do an online search to get his number. She wished now she would have thought to grab it before Shane had thrown her out the window. It had all her important contact information in it.

She waited patiently for the operator to connect her to the law offices of Decker and Marsh. It was just after three o'clock in the afternoon, and she hoped she'd be able to catch him in his office.

"Decker and Marsh," a perky receptionist answered. "How may I help you?"

"I need to speak with Galen Marsh. It's urgent."

"Mr. Marsh isn't taking calls right now. Can I take a message?"

"This is Rachel Valentine. I believe Mr. Marsh will take time to speak with me." Rachel heard a rustle of papers over the line and a few whispered voices. It must have been a new girl in the office.

"Hold please," the perky voice said.

Easy-listening music came over the line, and she waited less than a minute before her attorney answered the phone.

"Rachel," Galen Marsh said, his voice cracking. "Where have you been? I haven't heard from you in months."

Something was wrong. It was impossible to ignore the nervousness in his voice. Galen Marsh hadn't been thrilled when she'd "put him on her payroll" as he liked to call it. He never let an opportunity pass to remind her where she came from and that he thought no more of her than he had of her father. In Galen Marsh's eyes, anyone with the last name of Valentine should be locked behind bars. But it hadn't stopped him from taking her money. And despite his personal feelings about her family, she knew he wouldn't compromise his career by betraying her trust. It was just like she'd explained to Shane. Money talked, and there was such a thing as honor among thieves.

"What's going on, Galen?" Rachel asked, cutting right to the chase.

He sighed over the other end of the line, and she could imagine him shifting his considerable bulk behind the polished wood of his antique desk and reclining back in his chair. No doubt if he could have lifted his feet from the floor to the desk, they'd be propped there.

"You've got quite a few of your people looking for you, Rachel," he finally said.

"What do you mean, my people?"

"Your family. They seemed worried about you. Wanted me to let them know where to find you."

"You didn't tell them, did you?" she asked, panic evident in her voice.

"Of course not. Anyway, it's not like you've been keeping me up to date where you've been hiding."

"What's the problem then, Galen? And keep the lawyer speak to a minimum. Just the truth in a hundred words or less."

"It's just that they somehow found out that you've hired me." His voice had turned whiny and it was everything Rachel could do not to cringe at the petulant tone in his voice.

"And that bothers you because if they were able to find out I'm a client, then others might be able to find out as well. Am I right?"

"It's true I'd have preferred to keep our business relationship quiet. It won't make my other clients feel too comfortable when they're told that known criminals keep me on the payroll."

Rachel's voice turned icy and she wished she could have reached through the phone to strangle the pompous man on the other end. "As far as I know, Mr. Marsh, your clients don't include any criminals, known or otherwise. Make sure you relay the message. Am I clear?"

"Sure, sure," he said. "I just don't want any trouble. Your relatives make quite a statement, and I've got a family to think about."

"Just do your job and keep telling them you don't know anything," Rachel said.

"I *don't* know anything. Maybe you feel like enlightening me."

Rachel softened her voice and tried her best to add a little charm, but sometimes even she couldn't work miracles. "If you play your cards right, Mr. Marsh, you're going to be one of the most famous attorneys in the United States. I can guarantee you that much."

He laughed indulgently. "And how do you plan to pull that off, Ms. Valentine? Your father's as good as dead, so there's not much of a chance for me to put him behind bars where he belongs."

Rachel gritted her teeth and held back all the vile thoughts that came to her mind every time her attorney opened his mouth. "No, but you might have heard my uncle is controlling certain areas of the business now."

"Sure, but everyone knows it's only a matter of time before he's taken out. He doesn't have the charisma that Dom had. Word is there've been a few problems on the inside."

"Could be. I don't keep up with the family business. I have bigger fish to fry. Like catching the bastards who took my father before he was able to testify."

"Yeah, it's a damn shame they couldn't have gotten him after he spilled the information on all his rivals. It would have been a hell of a coup for the Justice Department. A victory all around."

"Exactly," Rachel said, hating the man more with every word that came out of his mouth. "I sent you a certified letter and a package several months ago with instructions to keep the package in a safe place and never open it. Do you have the package close by?"

"What's in that package, Rachel?"

"Do you have it close by?" she repeated.

"Yeah, it's in my office safe with all my own personal papers."

"Good. I need that package today. We're about half an hour from your office. I'll swing by and get it."

"No, I don't want you coming here. There have been too many people asking about you lately. I've already told them I don't know anything, but I'd hate to think of what they'd do to me if they thought I'd been lying all this time. The office closes at five. Meet me in the parking garage across the street at five thirty. I'll bring the package as long as you promise to find another attorney when this is all over. I'm too close to retirement to have to worry about looking over my shoulder every time a Valentine comes into town."

Rachel was silent for a few seconds. She wanted to demand he put the package in her hand now, but there was no reason not to wait and play things his way. She wasn't completely heartless, and she did understand his reasons for wanting to stay clear of her.

"Five thirty, Mr. Marsh," she finally agreed. "And I'm sure I don't have to remind you not to tell anyone of our conversation."

Rachel hung up and turned in her seat to look at Shane. She hadn't even noticed he'd parked the truck in an abandoned parking lot just off the highway.

"I take it there's no love lost between you and your attorney," he said with a smile.

"You could say that." Rachel hadn't realized how much tension had gathered in her shoulders once she'd heard the sound of Galen Marsh's voice. She slowly exhaled and stretched her sore muscles.

"He won't give us the package until office hours

are over," she said to fill the empty silence as Shane's gaze never left her. The pulse at the base of her throat began to flutter and her palms started to sweat. The man made her more nervous than anyone she'd ever met, and considering some of the people she'd known in her lifetime, that was saying something.

"Well, I guess we'll have to find something to do to fill the time," he finally said.

That's what she was afraid of.

What Rachel hadn't expected was a trip to the zoo.

"Excuse me, Mr. Hotshot Investigator, but I was under the impression we were running for our lives. Not taking a vacation."

Shane pulled a black ball cap out of his bag and put it on, along with a pair of dark sunglasses. "Has anyone ever told you that you need to have a little faith sometimes?"

"No, and if you'd come from my family you wouldn't have faith in anyone or anything other than yourself either."

"Good point," he acknowledged. "I need to make a call to someone at the FBI and see if he has any information that could be of use to us. I need to know who to contact once we make it to Chicago.

The zoo is always crowded, there are plenty of places to get lost if we need to, and do you see all of these towers surrounding us? They'll confuse the phone signal and give us a little extra time to get away if someone's listening in on my conversation."

"Do you think we lost the guy who shot at us in New Orleans?"

"I haven't noticed anyone tailing us, but it never hurts to be careful. I would never underestimate anyone who works for your family. They are professional and persistent."

"You seem to know a lot about my family."

Shane kept his face blank while wishing he could kick his own ass. It was in everyone's best interest for Rachel to never find out how well he knew the major players in her father's organization. "Everyone who has ever worked for the FBI knows something about your family," he hedged. He took her hand and led her into the zoo. "From what you told me about the conversation with your attorney, they could already have Marsh's phones tapped. Stay alert. If it is your uncle behind the attacks you might recognize someone."

"Doubtful. My father had more than two hundred employees, but I would bet that my Uncle Angelo has moved his own men up in the ranks. Just to ensure loyalty. It's what I would do."

They found a shaded spot near the elephants

that was relatively quiet, and Shane pulled out one of the disposable cell phones. He dialed a number that had a few too many digits and waited as he was connected to Washington, DC.

"I need to speak with Director Boyle. Tell him Shane Quincy is on the line."

"So the prodigal son returns," Harlan Boyle said after a few minutes. His voice was dark and rich like expensive chocolate, and a hint of the south still lingered no matter how hard he tried to get rid of it. "I knew you'd come back, boy. A man like you isn't meant to sit behind a desk."

Shane felt comfort in his old supervisor's words because he knew they were sincere. It hadn't been Harlan Boyle's fault that Shane's last job had turned into his own personal hell. Harlan Boyle had only been deputy director at the time. "Sorry to disappoint you, sir, but the desk suits me well."

"Doubtful, but I'll let you have your illusions. To what do I owe the honor of this phone call?"

"I have information on the Dominic Valentine situation. I need to know who the contact is in the Chicago office."

Director Boyle let out a low whistle. "That's a pie you don't want to stick your fingers in, son. People have a tendency to disappear when they know too much about the Valentines."

Shane glanced at Rachel out of the corner of his eye. Her dark head was tilted back against a shade tree, her eyes were closed and her breathing was slow and even. He would have thought she was asleep except for the way her hands were clamped together in a white-knuckled grip.

"I know, sir. But sometimes you just have to do what's right. I've got information that could potentially save a lot of people and a witness I'm trying to protect. There are very few people I can trust right now."

"I guess I should be flattered I'm on the short list," Harlan said. "But I'd prefer you not tell anyone you got the information from me. Director Shaw runs the Chicago office, and Special Agent Culver was one of his men. Shaw wasn't too happy to find Culver practically decapitated and fed to the fishes, and he's lost two other agents since then. You can imagine why no one works too hard to find where Dominic Valentine and his infamous list ended up."

"You think there's a leak on the inside?"

"They haven't found any evidence to prove it, and believe me, they've looked. I believe the agent who headed up the internal investigation is a buddy of yours. Jones Daugherty."

"You're kidding me? He's working IA?" Shane was speechless. Jones "Wildcat" Daugherty had been the team leader of the Alpha Squadron, a unit of seven men specialized in taking down terrorists. The Alpha Squadron had done two tours in Afghanistan together, but Shane had lost touch with everyone he'd served with after he'd left the FBI. The last he'd heard, Wildcat was climbing up the military career ladder.

"I can't see Wildcat Daugherty working for the FBI. Talk about someone who shouldn't be sitting behind a desk."

"Word around the Bureau is that he's damned good at it," Harlan said. "He's cleaned up a lot of messes in just a few months, but the Valentine situation isn't one of them."

"Thanks for the information, sir. I owe you one."

"I've got a job here for you whenever you're ready to come back."

"I don't owe you that much," Shane said with a laugh and hung up.

"Did you get the information you needed?" Rachel asked.

"Some of it. I don't want to make contact with the Chicago office until we're on the move again." Shane stood and stretched his muscles. He grabbed Rachel by the hand and pulled her into his arms, rubbing the knotted muscles at her shoulders.

"I don't mean to tell you how to do your job," she said, "but there's a man in a hat over there who seems awfully interested in us."

Shane pulled her closer so it looked as if they were embracing and whispered in her ear. "Yeah, it took him about five minutes to find us after I called my old headquarters."

"I thought the towers were supposed to give us a little time."

"Theoretically. But I know for sure now that Angelo has a plant inside the FBI. There's no other way they could have tracked us that fast otherwise."

"What are we going to do?" Rachel asked.

Shane took advantage of their situation by nipping lightly at her ear. She sucked in an unsteady breath, and he felt her quiver in his arms. "We're going to head to the food court and maybe check out a couple of those souvenir shops. Don't look at him and don't lose your cool. There's probably another man by the front gate."

A rush of adrenaline shot through his system, but he tamped it down. It was what he missed most about his previous jobs—the chase, the thrill of excitement, and the chance that only one man would be left standing in the end. Shane grabbed Rachel by the hand and they strolled to the food court, stopping to grab an ice cream on the way.

Shane picked up another follower out of the corner of his eye and squeezed Rachel's hand when she started to turn and look at him. "You've only got eyes for me, sugar."

"That's a hell of an ego you have."

"I'll be glad to back it up once we get out of here."

The sun was shining and Shane thought it was probably close to eighty degrees outside, but both men wore lightweight jackets to cover their shoulder holsters. Not good. The last thing he wanted to do was give them reason to open fire in such a crowded place.

Shane spotted several souvenir shops that were overrun with tour groups, and he gently pushed Rachel into the crowd. The air was cool inside the shops and sent chills over his sweat-slicked skin. Tables were filled to overflowing with T-shirts and knickknacks, so he took his cap off and put it on a display table and replaced it with a straw hat, hoping it would buy them some time. He didn't stop to look over his shoulder, though the itch at the back of his neck had turned into a burn. Shane picked up the pace when he saw an employee entrance behind one of the souvenir shops that led to a parking lot, and he kept Rachel in front of him, protecting her body with his own.

People scrambled and screams filled the air as the first sound of gunfire rang out behind him.

"Go, go!" he yelled to Rachel. "Stay low."

Wood splintered above Shane's head and a splinter sliced his cheek. Blood dripped steadily down his face, but he ignored it and kept his eye on the prize—a way out and their only chance for survival. He knocked over tables as he passed them and souvenirs littered the aisles.

Shane and Rachel pushed through the door at the back of the shop and the bright sun left tiny spots dancing in front of his eyes, but they forged ahead, adrenaline and instinct taking over. Another shot rang out and chips of concrete exploded in a cloud of dust at their feet.

"Almost there," Shane said, eyeing the gate of chain link that led into the employee parking lot at the back of the zoo. Sirens roared in the distance, overpowering the screams and sobs of the crowd behind him. Rachel ran full force into the gate and it swung open with a violent clang of metal hitting metal. The gate crashed behind him and he knew the men were hot on their heels.

"Keep running. Don't look back," he said to Rachel.

Shane hovered his body over hers and pushed her between a row of parked cars, forcing them both to their knees on the hot pavement. Rachel's breath was labored and her eyes were wide with fear, but she was hanging in there. Shane pulled a snub-nosed revolver from his ankle holster and listened as the footsteps of the men in pursuit slowed. There were still just two men, and Shane heard them split up so they could cover more ground.

The seconds ticking by seemed like hours and

he knew there would only be a short window of opportunity for them to escape. He and Rachel crawled between the cars, listening as the footsteps drifted closer, then farther away as the men crept up and down each aisle.

Shane slipped a small, thin tool from his pocket and went to work on the silver Taurus they were hiding beside. The lock snicked and he opened the door softly, pushing Rachel across the seat to the passenger side and then following her inside. He pushed her down, so she was hunkered on the floorboard, and he removed the plastic panel from the underside of the steering wheel.

The footsteps were getting closer again and sweat snaked down his spine as he touched bare wires together. The car rumbled to life and he pushed down on the accelerator. Tires squealed and the smell of burned rubber was overpowering as he shot out of the parking space. A bullet pinged off the back bumper and then another shattered a taillight. Shane pulled the driver's side door shut and sat up slowly as he put more space between them and the gunmen. He glanced in the rearview mirror and saw the men slow to a stop. One of them already had a cell phone in his hand, probably relaying the license plate of the car they'd stolen.

Rachel sat up in her seat and calmly fastened her seat belt once they were back on the highway.

"I guess we're going to be a few minutes late meeting Mr. Marsh."

Shane looked over at her. Her hair was mussed, her clothes were torn, and there was dirt smeared on the side of her face, but there was a sparkle in her eyes that told him she was glad to be alive.

"You're a hell of a woman, Rachel Valentine."

Chapter Five

Dusk was slowly creeping over the city by the time they'd found another vehicle. Smog was thick and glowed an eerie orange haze as the last rays of light disappeared. They'd found a green Ford Explorer in an overnight parking garage and taken it as a sign of luck. Traffic was congested as they wove their way down one-way streets and between skyscrapers, and Rachel breathed a sigh of relief as they got closer to her goal and freedom.

She'd had eight months to decide what she could do with her life once the axe hanging over her head had disappeared. New Orleans had felt like home from the moment she'd entered the city, and she knew it's where she would return. Maybe she'd even open her own design business. But those dreams were still a lifetime away.

"I had to leave the bag with my weapons and

most of the money in the pickup truck," Shane said, disturbing her private thoughts. The more she was around Shane Quincy, the more disturbing he became. He was an odd combination—all male, potently virile in a way that made women gravitate toward him, and his protective instincts only enhanced his appeal. But though those traits were attractive to Rachel, they weren't the ones that made her want to open herself to Shane Quincy like she had to no other man. He was wounded, a tortured soul, and Rachel recognized the symptoms in Shane only because she lived with them in herself.

"Did you hear me?" he asked. "We have little money and no guns."

"I have a feeling you're trying to tell me something," Rachel said, finally giving him her full attention.

"I'm telling you we have to get where we're going on the money I have in my pocket, or until I can get in touch with my friend and have him meet me with a few necessities. I don't want to take the chance of being seen by going back to the zoo and trying to retrieve the bag, and I especially don't want to bodyguard my client with a pissant .22 and six bullets."

"No, that doesn't really inspire a lot of confidence," she agreed. "Can't you have your office send you the things you need?"

"Anything they send can be easily traced. I've got good security, but people will be watching my office closely since your pal shot the hell out of it. My old squadron leader from the Marines will get us everything we need without alerting anyone."

The Explorer turned right at a stoplight and passed the offices of Decker and Marsh.

"There's the parking garage," Rachel pointed out. She looked at the clock on the dash and noticed it was past six o'clock. "I hope he's still waiting. He's not the most patient man, especially where I'm concerned."

"Looks like everyone has cleared out for the evening," Shane said.

The Explorer turned into the parking garage, and Rachel saw nothing but concrete and empty parking spaces. Thick pillars sat parallel to each other like stone soldiers as they drove up the ramps to each level.

"He's gone," she said, annoyed. "Why does he have to be so difficult? Would it have killed him to wait half an hour? I don't know how to get in touch with him out of the office. His home and cell number are in my phone back in New Orleans."

"That is a problem, sugar," Shane agreed.

Rachel watched as Shane unhooked the .22 from his ankle rig and put it on the console between them. "What's wrong? I don't see anyone following us."

They climbed higher. The shadows grew darker and dread settled in the pit of Rachel's stomach. There were too many places for one man to hide.

"It's my fault. I've been a little busy since your apartment caught fire yesterday, and I didn't ask all the questions I should have before we started out together. I guarantee whoever shot at us in New Orleans has already searched what's left of your apartment. They'll have your cell phone and any personal contacts you had in it, and they'll be searching for them."

"Oh my God, what have I done? I don't have many people's information in my phone because I don't have that many close friends, but my roommate from college and a friend who had the apartment across from mine in Chicago are in there. I have to call them and warn them."

"As soon as we get out of here," Shane promised.

Her Uncle Angelo was ruthless, and she prayed it wasn't too late to save Cleo's and Randy's lives. Angelo would leave no stone unturned until he had what he wanted.

They reached the top level of the parking garage and a lone black Mercedes was parked in the corner. The lights were dim and yellow and the Explorer's engine seemed excessively loud in the quiet.

"I don't know what kind of car he drives," Rachel said.

"Only one way to find out."

They parked the Explorer crosswise behind the Mercedes so they still had easy access to the exit.

"Leave your door open. Just in case," he told her.

Rachel got out of the car and met Shane around the other side. The .22 was down at his side and his expression was grim. When she looked at the car she understood why. Splatters of blood patterned across the windshield, and a body was hunched over the wheel.

It was a lot of blood.

"Stay back," Shane said and moved in front of her.

Rachel appreciated the gesture, but now wasn't the time to get squeamish. Now was the time to find the papers and get the hell out of Dodge. "That's him," she said as she walked around the car to get a better look at the victim's face.

"Good grief, Rachel. Do you ever listen?" he asked. "I told you to stay back."

"So I have to make you mad before you use my name instead of calling me sugar. Something I'll have to remember for the future. Let's get something straight, buttercup. I've hired you to protect my life, not my sensibilities. We have more important things to worry about besides whether or not I lose my lunch. I've got to find those papers."

"Whatever you say," Shane said, putting his hands up. "I always try to accommodate the client, since you're the one paying the bills."

Rachel couldn't help making him angry. It was better than breaking down in front of him and crying her eyes out, which was exactly what she wanted to do. She might be Dominic Valentine's daughter, but this was the first dead body she'd ever seen. And she hoped it would be the last.

"His briefcase is open on the passenger seat." Rachel reached for the door handle.

"Don't touch anything," Shane said tersely.

Rachel jerked her hand away from the door handle, surprised by the hardness in Shane's voice. She watched as he went back to the Explorer and dug around until he found a couple of tissues in the glove compartment.

"Thanks," she said as she took one from him. "I wasn't thinking about fingerprints."

"That's why you pay me the big bucks, sugar. We don't want to give local law enforcement a reason to look for us. If the FBI got wind of it, it would make things very difficult for the rest of our trip."

"Right. Because so far things have been a breeze," Rachel said testily. She was hurt by the harshness of his words and knew it was only a matter of time before she couldn't pretend that the sight of Galen Marsh didn't bother her. She used the tissue to open the door handle and found it unlocked.

The stench of death assaulted her as soon as she opened the door, and she held her arm in front of her mouth and nose to try to lessen it. But the cloying smell lingered in the back of her throat, no matter how hard she tried to get rid of it. She stepped back from the car and took a deep breath, focusing on what she had to do next.

Shane stood to the side, his expression challenging and devoid of all other emotion. It didn't look like he was going to offer a helping hand this time around. Well, she'd asked for it, though she hadn't thought he'd be able to cut off all his emotions like they were attached to a switch. She was Dominic Valentine's daughter. She could do anything she set her mind to.

Rachel held her breath and bent back into the car, careful not to touch the red stains that sat in liquid pools around the body. Marsh's briefcase lay open on the passenger seat and papers were scattered everywhere. All of them were splattered with blood. She made the mistake of looking at his face. His eyes were empty and stared straight at her, and his hair was matted with drying blood.

Rachel backed out of the car and collapsed to the ground, shoving her head between her knees as the little black dots began swimming in front of her eyes. She lost track of time as she tried to get herself under control, but she vaguely heard Shane sifting through papers, doing the job she should have been able to do.

"I don't see any envelopes," Shane said after a few minutes. "It looks like someone beat us to it, and now it's time for us to disappear."

Her stomach still felt queasy and she wasn't sure her legs would hold her if she tried to stand. "Shouldn't we call the police?"

"Not unless you want to go to jail. I wouldn't be surprised if this was a trap so we could be detained until your uncle's FBI insider can find us and do damage control. Get in the car."

Rachel let Shane help her to her feet and push her toward the Explorer. The sound of sirens was audible somewhere in the distance, and Shane didn't waste any time sticking around to find out.

Rachel barely had time to close her door and grab on to the door handle before Shane floored the Explorer. They sped down the narrow ramps at a neck-breaking pace and took the turns on two wheels. The squeal of tires echoed off the concrete walls, and they shot out of the garage onto the main road like a bullet out of a pistol.

The first squad car pulled into the garage, red and blue lights flashing and siren blaring, just as they turned the corner.

"You're insane," Rachel said, trying to control her breathing.

"Hey, it's all part of the bodyguard package. You're still alive aren't you?"

It was obvious Shane was still angry about the comment she'd made earlier. And if she wasn't mistaken, he wasn't just angry. He was hurt.

"Look, I'm sorry if I seemed ungrateful back there. I know you were just trying to help, but I've been on my own for a long time. I'm not used to white knights charging to the rescue, and it's obvious you have this need to save and protect when someone's in trouble. I'll be the first to admit I was wrong back there. I wasn't prepared for it, and I didn't handle it like I thought I'd be able to."

"You did okay, sugar. And I hate to disappoint you, but I'm nobody's white knight. Never have been. Never will be."

Rachel saw his jaw clench as he navigated them through the streets and back onto the highway. If she had dared to touch him, she knew he would have been cold as marble. What was going on in the mind of Shane Quincy? Was he really as heartless and detached as he wanted her to believe? She couldn't believe that she'd read him wrong after he'd risked his life saving her from the fire.

"Can we just agree that we're both approaching new territory and call a truce?" she finally said.

"Fine with me. I'd prefer to drop it if it's all the same to you. Marsh is dead, and as far as the list is concerned, it looks like we're on our way to Chicago," Shane said. "Unless you sent a copy to someone else."

"No one else has a copy."

Shane blew out a breath and smiled, his lips thin and hard. "Well, sugar, it looks like we're about to jump out of the frying pan and into the fire. And maybe we'll both come out alive."

"With an attitude like that, sugar," Rachel said with brow raised, "It's a wonder you have any clients at all."

Jimmy Grabbaldi waited until the dark green Explorer turned the corner before he started the engine of the nondescript beige Volvo he'd gotten from the rental company. Angelo Valentine was not happy with Jimmy's performance so far, and Jimmy was already dreading his punishment. Nobody screwed up Angelo Valentine's plans and got away with it. Not even one of his top men.

He'd lost Rachel and the private detective once they'd left New Orleans, and all he had to show for his efforts were sixteen stitches in the side of his cheek where he'd been cut by a piece of flying brick after Rachel had shot at him. She was going to have to pay for that. His only option had been to head back to her apartment and wait until the scene was clear so he could do a little investigating of his own. And he'd hit pay dirt.

He'd immediately called Angelo and told him what had happened. The silence on the other end of the line had sent chills down his spine. Angelo Valentine could say a lot without uttering a word. Angelo had ordered him back to Chicago and was going to send a more competent person in his place, and that's when Jimmy had told him what he'd found in Rachel's apartment.

He'd gotten her phone off the nightstand and found the list of people she trusted enough to stay in contact with, even though she was in hiding. There had only been three contacts in her address book, two friends and her attorney, and Jimmy had relayed the information to Angelo with satisfaction. There was no doubt in Jimmy's mind that any acquaintances of Rachel's would be "taken care" of.

In exchange for the information Jimmy provided, Angelo decided to let him continue his search for Rachel. The FBI informant who was working on the inside for the Valentine organization had relayed the information that Rachel and her new boyfriend had been in contact with an attorney who had access to the list. Jimmy's new assignment had been obvious, and he'd immediately headed to Dallas.

The freelance goons Angelo had hired had failed to kill Rachel and her boyfriend at the zoo, but Jimmy didn't worry too much about Rachel. Her time would come—just as Galen Marsh's had. Galen Marsh hadn't died with dignity. But more importantly, Marsh hadn't had a chance to give the list to Rachel.

Jimmy kept his eye on the Explorer in front of him as they merged into traffic on the highway headed north. He hit the speed dial on his phone and turned it on speaker.

"Mr. Grabbaldi. I hope you're calling me with good news." Angelo Valentine had the voice of a demon. It was the only thing Jimmy could think of as sweat pooled at the base of his neck and ran in rivulets down his temples. Angelo's voice was low and gravelly due to a throat injury he'd suffered as a young man, but there was nothing weak about it.

"Yes, sir. I've picked up Rachel Valentine and her friend in Dallas just as the informant told you. They're headed north. I'll wait until they stop for the night to take them out."

"Good, good. And what about the other little problem? I assume you had no problems with that job."

"Mr. Marsh is taken care of, sir, and the papers have been recovered."

"Excellent, Mr. Grabbaldi. Destroy them immediately. I may decide to let you live after all." There was a pause over the line and Jimmy could hear Angelo breathing. "Then again, maybe not."

"Yes, sir," Jimmy said as the spit dried up in his mouth, making it difficult to swallow.

"Don't let them get to Chicago, Mr. Grabbaldi. Rachel Valentine has another copy of the list somewhere. Don't fail me."

The line went dead and Jimmy deliberately relaxed his cramping fingers from around the steering wheel. Rachel Valentine was headed into Oklahoma. It was the quickest way to get across the border and lose the interest of any local law enforcement. He knew from experience that Rachel and her private detective would be stuck on a two-lane road for hours. He'd have to be careful not to be seen.

Jimmy turned the radio on the classical station to soothe his nerves and plan his future. He had a nice fat bank account in the Caymans, and he figured it was time for Jimmy Grabbaldi to retire. Killing Rachel Valentine would be his last job. He wasn't going to tempt fate and give Angelo the chance to change his mind about letting him live.

Chapter Six

Shane waited in the car and kept an eye on Rachel as she used a payphone to call her friends. By the agitated way she kept wrapping the phone cord around her wrist, it didn't look like she was having a lot of luck reaching them. If Angelo Valentine had put a hit out on Rachel's friends, Shane felt sure they didn't have much of a chance for survival. But he wasn't going to be the one to say so.

They were stopped at a gas station on the Texas/Oklahoma border. It was the last place to get gas for more than two hours, but Shane had another reason for stopping. He wanted to see if the beige sedan he'd spotted in his rearview mirror was really following them. Shane tried to get a good look at the driver, but the sedan motored past them without giving them a glance.

Rachel got back into the Explorer and Shane

thought she looked close to tears. She'd had a rough twenty-four hours, and it wasn't over yet. Neither of them had slept and their clothes were torn and dirty.

"You can try to call them again once we find a place to stay for the night," Shane said.

"I know. It's just that they're clueless as to what I've gotten them involved in, and they have no way of protecting themselves. It was stupid of me not to cut all ties completely, but I couldn't face leaving everything and everyone I've ever known behind all at once."

Her words struck a chord with Shane. Wasn't that exactly what he'd done after his wife had died and he'd left the FBI? He hadn't spoken to any of his friends since the funeral. Wildcat, Dixon, Cutter, Jax, Doc, and Merlin—men who had guarded his back and been there for him in the toughest of times. He'd turned his back on them all. He'd packed up his meager belongings and left Washington without looking back. He'd picked New Orleans simply by closing his eyes and pointing to a place on the map. It had only been coincidence that he'd grown up in a town not too far from the city. And it was fortunate because the deep south and the swamps didn't accept outsiders. Doors opened for him and his business because his mama had been an Arceneaux, and names meant everything in New Orleans.

His blood family was gone, but the men who'd been closer than brothers to him still lived. Guilt and shame crept its way over him and he promised himself he'd make amends and reach out to them as soon as Rachel Valentine was safe.

It was full dark as they crossed the border and headed north through Oklahoma. The silence was heavy, each of them lost in their own thoughts. Shane figured it would be close to midnight by the time they reached Tulsa. It was the closest city he knew of that would have a place to eat and an available motel. It was risky stopping for the night, but Rachel couldn't go on much longer. And even though he could go on as long as the mission required, sleep and food would fuel his body and keep him alert.

"Did you get in touch with your FBI friend?" Rachel asked, breaking the silence.

That was another reason Shane had wanted to stop before they entered a new state. He knew his calls to Jones Daugherty at FBI Headquarters in Chicago would be traced. And he'd been right. He'd heard the clicks on the other end of the line that told him the call was being traced, and as soon as Wildcat had come on the line the conversation had been short and sweet.

"Yeah, I used the payphone while you were in the bathroom. Jones gave me a private number to call as soon as we get to a place I can talk for a while. He could tell I was in a hurry and needed to get off the line before they could pinpoint a location."

"Don't take this the wrong way, but are you sure you can trust this guy? How do you know he isn't the informant working on the inside for Uncle Angelo?"

"Some things you just know. Wildcat has saved my life on more than one occasion and I've saved his. I'd trust him with my life and yours too. He's good people."

"I guess that's good enough for me," she said.

"Why don't you try to get some sleep," Shane said. "We've got a long drive ahead of us."

"Are you kidding me? As soon as we crossed the border into Oklahoma I've felt like we were in that movie."

"Lost Highway?"

"No, *Deliverance*. I haven't seen a town, a streetlight, a restaurant or another car for hours. It's like we've entered into the Twilight Zone. And I don't mean to be a pest, but I haven't eaten anything since lunch and I'm starving. I know you're a macho tough guy and could probably sustain yourself by picking grass from the side of the road, but us weaklings have to have real sustenance."

"Like a cheeseburger?" Shane asked, laughing

as her stomach picked that moment to rumble loudly.

"Yeah, a cheeseburger would be good."

"We'll be in Tulsa before too long. We can stop there and grab a bite to eat before bunking down for the night."

Shane settled back into comfortable silence and looked out into the night. He'd been all over the world, and it always amazed him to see how different the sky looked. He'd been in third world countries and drug-run jungles, but he'd never seen a sky as black as the one over him right now. No stars shone and the moon was just a sliver of pale dust. The land wasn't cluttered with modern technology—no oil wells, power lines, self-service gas stations or cell phone service. It was just open, empty land.

Almost an hour had passed in silence when Rachel sat up in her seat and emitted a sound he'd not heard from her before. He was already checking the rearview mirror and increasing their speed, his gun clutched comfortably in his right hand while he searched for danger.

"Oh, my God," she said, pulling on his shirt sleeve like a child. "Do you see it?"

"See what?" he asked, wondering if she was hallucinating because of lack of sleep.

"The lights. All the glorious lights," she said. "Stay with me, Quincy. The lights mean there's civilization—food, a shower, a soft bed. Don't tell me you're not excited about the prospects that lie ahead of us. Tulsa is my new favorite city."

Shane didn't want to think about Rachel Valentine and a soft bed in the same sentence together. Which posed another problem. He was going to have to share a room with her. Pure torture. She'd been to hell and back in the last twenty-four hours and looked like it, and she was still the only woman who'd woken the dead places inside of him. Being a professional was going to kill him.

"Step on it, sugar," she said. "Your client is hungry and in desperate need of a shower. And you did say you always try to please the client."

"Yes, ma'am," Shane said. He was lighter of heart than he'd been in a long time, and it was all because he was on the run from a madman with a woman he was afraid he could fall in love with. It was fortunate he had no plans to go down that path, or he'd be in real trouble.

Rachel's stomach rumbled again as Shane pulled into the lot of a twenty-four-hour diner attached to what could at best be called a "seedy" motel—minus the "M." Jake's otel was as basic as you could get. It was a rectangle of sandy-colored, crumbling brick trimmed with turquoise paint. There were two floors and twenty-four rooms with stairs at each end, and each room had one window. A soft drink machine sat in the middle of the sidewalk with an "out of order" sign taped to it.

"You sure know how to show a girl a good time, Quincy."

"That's what they tell me. But this will have to do until Jones can supply me with some more cash."

"My eyes are going to be closed anyway, so it's not like I'll actually see the roaches crawling around on the floor."

"That's the spirit," he said.

They got out of the Explorer and headed toward the diner. "It's getting cooler," Rachel said, rubbing her bare arms.

The wind had picked up and the air smelled of ozone and static lay heavy in the air. "Looks like we'll get a thunderstorm before the night's over. I hope Jake's otel can handle a little rain."

The diner was empty when they went inside. Fluorescent lights flickered overhead and cracked vinyl booths with scarred Formica tabletops lined the walls. The floor was black and white checked squares, dingy with what looked like years of scuff marks and soda spills.

A lone waitress with bottle-thick glasses and permed brown hair that frizzed away from her face sat perched on a stool behind the register. Her age was somewhere between thirty-five and sixty-five. The lights weren't flattering. She was doing a crossword puzzle and gave them no more than a cursory glance when they entered. Her sigh of annoyance could be heard all over the restaurant.

"How you folks doin' tonight," she said as she grabbed a couple of greasy menus and led them to a corner booth.

"Fine, thank you," Rachel said politely.

"The name's Nadine. Coffee's fresh and bottomless if you want it. Or we got other stuff."

"Coffee's fine with me," Shane answered.

"Just water for me," Rachel said. "And I already know I want the biggest cheeseburger you have with a side of fries."

"Make that two," Shane said, before the waitress had a chance to lay the greasy menu in front of him.

"Comin' right out, folks," Nadine said and shuffled away.

"I'm going to wash up in the bathroom and see if I can find a phone to use," Rachel said. "I won't rest easy until I get in touch with Cleo and Randy and know they're safe."

Shane waited until she disappeared and moved to a position where he could see both the bathroom and the front doors. The parking lot was still empty other than the green Explorer, but he didn't want to take any chances. He pulled out a slip of paper from his wallet that held the number Jones had given him earlier that evening and he used one of the disposable cell phones.

"What the hell have you gotten involved in, Ace?" Jones Daugherty asked as he came on the line. Ace had been Shane's call name in the Marines because of his ability to hit his target with complete accuracy.

"Your name's come up with a red flag all over the FBI. Word has it your apartment building was torched, your business was destroyed and you're wanted for questioning as a person of interest in the murder of a high-profile attorney in Dallas. And all because of a woman. Sounds like you should have stayed in the FBI. Going independent has obviously made you forget how to follow the rules."

"Yeah, well, you shouldn't listen to gossip. And I was never that good at following rules, anyway."

"I know that better than anyone," Jones said with a laugh.

"As far as what you've heard, my apartment wasn't damaged in the fire, it was my neighbor's. Insurance will cover the damage to my business and somebody else had already killed the lawyer before we got there. But I can confirm a hundred percent that it all happened because of a woman."

"Tell me," Wildcat ordered.

"Rachel Valentine is in my protection, and let's

just say that her uncle doesn't think that's such a good idea. And after our trip to Dallas, I'm beginning to think someone in the FBI doesn't think it's such a good idea either."

Nothing but silence greeted Shane from the other end. "You still there, Wildcat?"

"I've done an internal investigation on every agent in the Bureau who was ever involved with the Valentines. You know how big that list is. You were on the original task force."

Shane winced. "Don't remind me."

"I've found no evidence that there's someone working for Angelo Valentine on the inside. And believe me, I've looked. I've looked hard."

"Just keep your eyes open."

"Roger that. Where are you now?"

"We're in Tulsa for the night, but we'll head out early in the morning. I've got to figure out some way to get Rachel to the bank in Chicago and get the papers out of her lockbox before anyone knows we're there."

"Fat chance of that happening. I've heard it through the grapevine that people are expecting you to show up here eventually. You'll have to be a ghost to get past Angelo's men, not to mention the FBI alert that's out on you."

"I don't suppose you'd be inclined to help an old friend?" Shane asked.

"What, and risk losing this glamorous job? I

could probably be persuaded to help you out. But it'll cost you. And you might not like the favor when it comes down to it."

"You always were a perverse bastard," Shane said. "But you leave me with no choice but to agree. And look on the bright side. If you get fired I'll even find a place for you on my staff. My secretary is getting close to retirement. How are your typing skills?"

Shane smiled as Jones laughed and uttered a crude suggestion. "In all seriousness, Wildcat, I really appreciate your help. You don't owe me anything. I haven't exactly been the greatest friend over the last couple of years, but I'm grateful all the same."

"What the hell kind of Dr. Phil psychobabble is that? I expect a man is inclined to go off on his own every now and then. There are some things in the world that change and some things that don't. Try to remember that. Now tell me what you need me to do."

Shane felt the grip of guilt release around his heart. He'd been afraid his lack of interest in his friends, hell, his lack of interest in life, after his wife's death had screwed things up with Wildcat past the point of no return. But Wildcat was acting like the years hadn't passed at all, and Shane was grateful.

"Well, for starters, I need guns and plenty of

ammunition. I'll also need a couple of flak jackets and infrared goggles. You know what I prefer. And I need enough cash to buy basic supplies and get us where we need to go."

"Anything else?" Jones asked.

"I need to take a look at the files you've collected on each agent working the Valentine case. The insider is there somewhere, and Rachel will never be safe as long as that person is running around. I also need a safe house if you've got one available close enough to Chicago so the trip can be made in less than an hour. It'll give us a place to stay until I figure out what the hell we're going to do."

"If anyone finds out about this you know my ass is grass," Jones said, "but I'll see what I can do. Give me till noon tomorrow. You should be able to make it to St. Louis, Missouri, by then if you leave at dawn. I'll meet you in the parking lot of the Galleria just outside of Nordstrom. They're doing a lot of construction and the lot will be crowded. I'll be in a black Tahoe."

The line went dead and Shane slipped the phone into his pocket. Rachel took her seat across from him and he could tell by the look on her face that she still hadn't been able to get in touch with her friends.

"No luck?" he asked. Nadine took that moment to deliver their cheeseburgers and refill his coffee.

"No, just an answering machine at both places. I didn't leave a message."

Shane took a bite of his food. Grease dripped onto his plate, and he watched Rachel try to avoid the same problem by cutting hers in half. Grease dripped down her chin and onto her arm at the first bite.

"I don't want to hear a word," she said, laughing. "I'm hungry enough to not care about what's in this burger."

When they were finished Shane pulled out his wallet and left enough to cover the check and a tip. "Let's see what our neighborhood motel has to offer."

They walked outside to the Explorer and drove around the diner and the motel to the front office. The city was silent and the streets empty. Cars were scattered sporadically in the parking lot, enough to tell Shane that Jake's otel probably did a lot of business by the hour. A lone streetlight glowed yellow in the parking lot, and a flashing neon sign declared vacancies.

Lightning streaked across the sky and the first rumbles of thunder grumbled in the distance.

Shane opened the cracked glass door of the office and ushered Rachel in front of him. The smell of stale cigarettes and burned coffee was overwhelming. A small black-and-white TV sat in the corner with foil wrapped around the antennae and the volume turned all the way down. A man sat in a threadbare recliner and didn't take his eyes away from the screen as the bell rang above the door.

"Excuse me," Shane said as the man continued to sit in his chair and stare at the TV. "We'd like a room for the night."

"It's thirty-seven fifty for the night. Twenty for an hour. Sign your name in the book, and take a key off the hook. Checkout's at eleven."

Sometimes things worked out the way they were supposed to, Shane thought. He wouldn't even have to bribe the man to keep their names out of the register. Shane left two twenties on the counter and didn't bother signing the book. He took the key off the hook for the room at the very end on the bottom floor. Room number twenty-three. It was hidden behind two large dumpsters and would give them a little coverage if they had to make a sudden exit.

Shane didn't bother to thank the guy as they left the musty office. He left the Explorer parked where it was so as not to give their room location away and grabbed a small sack of toiletries and two clean shirts (one in each of their sizes) he'd bought when he'd stopped at the Walmart in Texas to buy clothes for Rachel.

"I don't suppose you've got clean sheets in that little sack, do you?" Rachel asked.

"Nope. Toothbrushes, toothpaste, soap, shampoo, a hairbrush, deodorant and clean shirts. No sheets."

"Darn. I hate to tell you this, but I don't think I'm brave enough to stay in Jake's otel. Maybe we could find a nice cardboard box in an alley somewhere."

"Think of it as an adventure. If you can survive the night here, then you can survive the mob." Shane stuck the key in the lock and pushed open the door. The air inside the room was stuffy and stale. He flicked on the light switch and immediately wished he could take back the action.

"I've always thought hot pink and turquoise complement each other," Rachel said.

Shane shut the door behind him and immediately locked the deadbolt and put on the chain. He pulled the curtains closed so no outside glare from the streetlights was let in. "What about the brown-and-orange bedspread. What does that complement?" he asked.

"I'm not sure that bedspread would complement the flames I'd like to burn it with."

The room was barely large enough to hold the furniture inside. A large king-size bed dominated the room and a small table and chairs sat in the corner. A small door led into a closet-sized bathroom and there were hooks on the wall to hang clothes instead of a closet.

Shane went about turning the fan on and putting the toiletries in the bathroom, noticing that Rachel still stood in front of the door chewing on her bottom lip. She was staring at the king-sized bed like it was leading her down the path to hell, and he had to bite the inside of his cheek to keep from laughing when she spotted the circular mirror on the ceiling.

He knew exactly what she was feeling because the bed had given him more than a moment of concern, but as long as he remembered that she was a client and he was being paid to protect her, all thoughts of wanting to make love to her disappeared. Or at least mostly disappeared. He'd have to be dead not to think of it a little.

"Why don't you go ahead and take the first shower? You look dead on your feet," he said while he unhooked his ankle holster and put the .22 on the nightstand closest to the door.

"Yeah, okay," she said, still staring at the bed. "So I guess you're planning for both of us to sleep there."

"Unless you want to sleep in the tub. Don't worry, your virtue will stay intact. I never take advantage of a client."

"So I guess the kiss you gave me earlier was saying something like, 'Way to go, pal,'" she said with a raised eyebrow and quirk of lips.

"Just take your shower. We've got to be up at dawn and on our way to St. Louis."

"I take it your friend has agreed to help us?"

"Yes. He'll have everything we need and give us a place to stay for a couple of days while we're trying to figure out the mess of how to get you to Chicago in one piece. Don't use all the hot water," Shane said and lay back on the bed fully clothed.

Rachel went into the bathroom and grimaced at the avocado-green fixtures. At least the color probably hid the mold well. A dingy shower curtain hung limply from a tarnished rod and she jerked it open quickly, expecting to see either a knife-wielding maniac or a spider the size of her fist. She blew out a breath of relief when she saw neither.

Rachel took her clothes off in the tub so she wouldn't have to stand in her bare feet on the grimy tile and folded her ruined clothes over the back of the toilet. She turned the water on and was thankful that at least the hot water worked and came out of the shower nozzle in more than a trickle. If she closed her eyes, she was pretty sure standing in the moldy shower of Jake's otel was the best experience she'd had in a long time.

Fatigue was starting to take its toll, so she washed her hair and body quickly and then turned the water off. A rod on the wall held two paper-thin towels, so she grabbed one and dried her body quickly and then wrapped the towel around her sopping head. She washed her underwear in the sink and hung it to dry over the rod and slipped on the plain white T-shirt Shane had bought her. It barely covered her backside, but it was the only thing she had to sleep in. Sleeping next to Shane was enough temptation in itself. What she really needed was full body armor and a chastity belt.

Rachel left the light on in the bathroom and made her way to her side of the bed quickly, slipping under the covers before Shane had a chance to glance in her direction. She didn't know that Shane had noticed everything about her—how the shirt clung to her damp body or how long her legs were.

She fell asleep blissfully unaware that she was torturing her protector.

Chapter Seven

The late afternoon sun baked the city and tortured pedestrians as they scurried to their destinations. Washington was in the middle of a heat wave, the hottest the city had seen in years, and beads of sweat ran down Shane's temples and into his eyes—the salt stinging and the sun glaring.

The Federal Reserve Building on Constitution Avenue was full of people just after lunch—tour groups, employees, and government officials. He was positioned on top of the Roosevelt Building across the street. Black tar from the roof stuck to his clothes and his rifle was set on a tripod stand aimed at the building. He had a perfect view to the inside of the building through his scope.

The gunman had gathered all of the hostages and made them sit in the center of the room, legs crossed and hands flat on the floor. It had only taken a glance through the scope to see the people were terrified—children from a tour group sat huddled in fear and the men and women around them tried to offer comfort and dry their tears.

His wife stood out like a beacon. An authority figure who was in complete control, though he could tell by the way she rubbed her hands on her black skirt that she was nervous. But she didn't show her captor fear. Her posture was straight and defiant and her expression angry as she followed the gunman's every movement.

A negotiator was called in to speak with the gunman, but the standard tactics weren't working. The gunman was becoming more agitated with every call. He paced back and forth across the marble tile like a caged animal, the people at his feet forgotten and his demands growing stronger. Minutes turned into hours and the heat intensified as the sun crept higher.

A car alarm blared from down the block and a chopper circled overhead. The smell of hot tar and exhaust made the inside of his nose raw as he looked through the scope of his rifle. The streets were cordoned off around the building. The gunman had asked for an armored truck to load gold bars into, and it sat big and black and shiny in front of the Federal Reserve Building. The gunman picked hostages to load the truck and then had them return to the bank and sit back down on the floor.

The gunman grabbed a woman from the floor and used her as a shield as he began to leave the building. From all appearances, it looked like he was going to let the other hostages go.

"Fire when ready," Director Hudson ordered Shane. "I don't want the bastard to step foot outside of that building. We don't need any more of a media circus than we've already got."

"What about the hostage?" Shane asked, his voice hollow.

"Take the shot, Quincy," Director Hudson ordered again, and Shane knew the life of the woman wasn't as important as the bigger picture to a man like Hudson.

But Shane followed orders. His finger was steady on the trigger as he slowly pulled it back. The rifle jerked in his arms and the bullet cut through the waves of heat pouring up from the pavement as if it were in slow motion. The gunman was unsuspecting, his focus on the struggling woman and getting them both to the truck.

The other hostages were restless and beginning to stand, relieved the ordeal was over. The crack of the rifle firing was delayed, the bullet faster than the speed of sound, and Shane watched as it sliced through the glass doors of the Federal Reserve and into the gunman's heart, missing the woman by only a fraction of an inch. But in the end it hadn't mattered. She'd died anyway.

Real time whooshed back in an instant as the man fell to his knees. The city was still, a void in space, and then all hell broke loose. The explosion rocketed through the front of the building, engulfing it in black smoke and flame. Debris rained from the sky and large chunks of concrete catapulted into the street, damaging cars and breaking the windows of the surrounding buildings. The lives of so many people had meant less than the 400-ounce rectangles of precious metal.

Shane's life as he'd known it had ended in an instant.

He woke gasping for air and his skin slicked with sweat. He was disoriented and cold and his muscles cramped. And when a soft hand touched him on the shoulder he had to fight to keep from jumping out of the bed like a coward.

"Shane?" Rachel asked.

He didn't answer her. Couldn't answer her. The soft hand began rubbing slow circles over his back until his breathing slowed. Rain pounded against the window and thunder cracked loudly, shaking the glass.

"Shane? Are you okay?" she asked again.

"Yeah, just give me a minute." The dream was always the same. He'd killed his wife. Killed all of those people. The children. Despite the higher-ups who had given him the order to fire, it had been only his finger on the trigger. Not theirs.

"Do you want to talk about it?"

Shane laughed sardonically and rubbed his hands across his face. "Hell, no. I lived it. Why would I want to talk about it? You sound like one of the FBI shrinks."

He was churned up, feeling mean and nasty, and he desperately wanted a bottle of Jim Beam. But he'd given up the hard stuff and taken up running instead. And now he was stuck in a motel room with a woman who made him crazy and neither of his vices were available.

Shane lay back down and turned onto his side, facing away from Rachel. The sweat on his skin was drying, leaving him clammy and cold. Rachel's fingers were driving him to distraction. He'd never considered sex as a way to chase away the bad dreams, but he was beginning to think it might not be a bad idea to take up a third vice just in case he was ever in a situation like this one again.

He hadn't touched a woman in two years, and the need rose up in him swiftly. His senses were heightened—the smell of her skin and the way her breath feathered across his cheek. She snuggled up close behind him, her hand continuously soothing, while his body coiled with tension. Would she continue to soothe him if he decided to use her body to rid himself of his frustrations? He couldn't do that to her. Couldn't do it to anyone. No one deserved to be treated that way. Which led him back to running or Jim Beam. He choked on a laugh, but it was a sob that caught in his throat.

"I always hear you leave your apartment in the middle of the night," she said, breaking the silence. "Where do you go?"

"Running through the city. It's beautiful at night," he said, trying to think of anything but the touch of her hand or her softness pressed against him. "I tried drowning myself in alcohol for a few months, but I didn't like that version of me when I looked in the mirror any more than the version I see now. So I poured the bottles down the drain and stopped looking at myself in the mirror altogether. I didn't realize my sleep habits kept you awake."

"I'd try to stay awake until you came back, just so I could listen to you play the piano for a while. Such sad music comes out of you, Shane. Sometimes it would make me cry."

"Well, the blues aren't meant to be happy."

"No, I suppose not, but I enjoyed hearing you all the same. You have strong hands," she said, running her fingers down the length of his arm to the tips of his fingers.

His hands were rough and his fingers calloused, but she was right. They were strong. If only the rest of his body and mind could live up to the potential. The tension slowly drained from his body with every gentle stroke of her hand. It was a comfortable feeling to wake up beside a woman in the middle of the night. He'd forgotten the intimacy, the feeling of knowing a lover's touch or the sighs that said they were dreaming peacefully. The vise around his chest loosened and he was able to breathe easier. And before he could help himself, the words started pouring out of his mouth.

"I killed my wife," Shane said, expecting Rachel to recoil. To slap him or gasp in horror. She did neither. She just listened.

Rachel felt sick inside. What kind of horrors had Shane been living with? She didn't believe for a moment that he'd killed his wife. He was too honorable—too loyal. He was a protector of the innocent, and his basic characteristics would never let him be anything else.

So when he dropped the bombshell about his wife, she listened with an open mind while her heart broke over the tragedy. He told her of his nightmares, and how he relived those last moments night after night, shouldering the blame for something he'd had no control over. And she listened with envy as he spoke of the woman he'd loved—

her beauty, her strength and her faith in him that he was making a difference in the world.

"I've spent my entire adult life obeying someone else's orders—in the Marines and then again in the FBI," Shane said. "I've always been a pawn in someone else's game. What does that say about me that I never stopped to think for myself? That I just followed the orders of others so blindly without first thinking of all the consequences?"

"I'd say it made you the best person to do your job. The job does not define the man, Shane. You're still your own person, with your own beliefs and priorities. And no one can fault you for doing what you had to do in those last seconds."

"Well, they did fault me. And I can't blame them."

"Trying to relive history, to rethink the outcome of situations, will never give you peace. You can't say for certain that he wouldn't have detonated the bomb strapped to his chest anyway. He was a sociopath. It was he who was responsible for the loss of all those lives. Not you. There are a hundred different scenarios that could have played out that day, and they all could have ended badly. From the way you described your wife I'd think she wouldn't be too happy with the way you're blaming yourself. What would she say?"

She'd probably tell him to stop moping and get the job done. "I don't know, but every day I pray that she would have forgiven me if she was still alive. She was strong. Stronger than me. Everything was black and white with Maggie. Right or wrong. There were no gray areas to get lost in. It seemed I was always skirting the gray areas in my line of work, and she'd just give me that look that said, 'Suck it up and do what's right.'"

"She sounds like an amazing woman," Rachel said.

"She was. A day doesn't go by that I don't think of her. She's my conscience. And loving her taught me something very important. That emotions always cloud the issues. I'll never let myself love anyone as wholeheartedly as I did her. The body's not meant to withstand that much torture, that much loss. It's okay to put yourself into work and relationships, but there's no reason for them to matter too much. It can only lead to disaster."

The first tear snaked down Rachel's cheek before she could stop it. Her hand had stilled on his and her breath was caught in her throat. What had she been thinking, dragging Shane into a mess of her own making and then becoming attached to him? He was everything a real man should be—honorable and trustworthy and honest. And he continued to be that way despite the pain that weighed him down. She was past the point of where she could lie to herself. She was falling in love with him. But she had to remind herself it wasn't real. These were tense times and he was her protector. A psychologist would have a field day with her attraction to him.

"Maggie would have forgiven you," she finally said, but he didn't hear her. His breathing had steadied under her hand and she realized he'd fallen asleep, the nightmares purged from his soul with his confessions. But Rachel was wide awake. And more alone than she'd ever been. She rolled away from Shane and curled into a ball, letting the tears fall silently. It was the first time she'd cried since she was a child. And all because she was in love—no, infatuation—with a man who would never love her in return.

She'd stay with Shane Quincy until the papers were safely in the possession of the FBI, and then tell him goodbye with a confidence and bravado that had come from years of practice and guidance from her father. And then she'd never look back.

Chapter Eight

Rachel woke the moment Shane left the bed. She'd spent the night tossing and turning, a deep sleep eluding her for uncomfortable dreams and thoughts of the man beside her.

The bed dipped and rose and she opened her eyes. The room was still pitched in darkness and no glimmer of morning light peeked underneath the curtains. Shane flicked on the bedside lamp and she watched the muscles in his back flex as he reached toward the ceiling in a stretch that left her mouth watering. A pair of snug boxer-briefs hugged his hips, his hair was mussed, and a day's worth of beard shadowed his face. He wasn't making it easy for her to stick to her plan.

He pulled on his clothes and strapped the .22 back to his ankle, checking the cylinder even though the amount of bullets in the chamber hadn't changed since the day before. He moved around the room silently, packing up their meager belongings. He reminded her of a big cat, the way he moved so efficiently, almost lazily, but the power was coiled just beneath the surface. Always ready.

"Rise and shine, sugar," he said. "I want to be out of here before light hits. We're supposed to meet Wildcat in St. Louis at noon."

"I'm awake. And don't call me sugar," Rachel said, her mood dark as she shuffled into the bathroom to get dressed. She threw on her clothes, washed her face, brushed her teeth, and pulled her hair back into a ponytail. The bags under her eyes spoke of a sleepless night and her skin was pale against the harsh lighting in the bathroom. She probably wouldn't have to worry about any more kisses from Shane.

Shane was standing by the door impatiently by the time she emerged from the bathroom, and he avoided making eye contact with her. Tension hung thick in the air between them, and words spoken in the dark of night lay heavy on both their minds.

Rachel noticed the .22 in Shane's hand.

"Stay behind me and to my right. The dumpsters will give us good coverage until we can make it to the Explorer. You ready?"

"As I'll ever be."

Shane opened the door and she followed close behind him. It took a minute for her eyes to adjust to the darkness, but it didn't look like Jake's otel had changed much over the last few hours. The thunderstorm had turned into a light mist and water filled the holes in the parking lot. If it was possible, Jake's otel looked even more pitiful than it had the night before, soggy and neglected.

They were behind the dumpsters and Rachel's pulse picked up as she thought of how long they'd be an open target on the way to the car. Her Uncle Angelo could have men placed anywhere—on the rooftops, under cars, or at the liquor store across the street. She didn't like the thought of Shane putting himself in front of her. Weren't two sets of searching eyes better than one? She tried to move around him so she could see, but he stubbornly kept his body in front of hers as they edged out from behind the dumpsters.

The fine hairs on her arms and the nape of her neck prickled a moment before the gunshot rang out. Shane pushed her to the ground and into the wet, covering her body with his own. She felt his body jerk against her and they went down hard, bodies tangling. Her elbows cracked against the concrete and the breath whooshed out of her lungs, making it impossible for her to draw in a breath. Shane dropped the gun seconds before his head bounced off the pavement and his body went limp on top of hers.

Two more shots pinged off the dumpster and

another hit the brick just over her head, sending shards flying.

"Shane! Shane, wake up," she said. He was dead weight on top of her and she pushed with all her might to roll him over.

He groaned as she rolled him to his side, and she could already see the lump forming on his temple. Rachel pushed to her hands and knees and felt around the knot. It was then she noticed the blood as it ran in rivulets down his arm and joined the puddles of water on the sidewalk.

"Oh, my God. Shane," she said, tapping him lightly on the side of the cheek.

"Stop beating on me, woman. I'm fine. Just a knock on the head." His eyes were open now but he still looked a little unsteady.

"Oh, yeah? What about the bullet in your arm?"

He looked down at his left shoulder in surprise. "Hell. We don't have time for this. At least it looks like the bullet went all the way through."

It looked like he was losing a lot of blood to Rachel, and his hand shook as he tried to apply pressure to the wound.

"It's no big deal," he said between gritted teeth. "The shooter must have had a night scope to have such a clear shot, but the sun's starting to come up. The direction of the sun's in our favor. There will be a glare for a few minutes as he adjusts. He'll change positions and try to trap us behind here. It's what I would do in the same situation. I need to get a pinpoint on his location and take him out. Otherwise, we're going to be sitting ducks. If something happens to me I want you to run for the car and get out of here. I'll try to stall him as long as I can."

The .22 lay on the ground. Shane's voice was getting weaker and his pupils were large and black.

"Like hell," Rachel said. "We're in this together, Quincy." She grabbed the gun from the ground and crouched low.

"Where are you, you son of a bitch?" she yelled. Shane grabbed for her, but she dodged his hand easily.

Her heart was racing and her mind was on Shane, but she knew she had to pull it together so they could both escape alive. Rachel slowed her breathing and cleared her mind like she'd been taught. It wouldn't help to think that the target was a live human being instead of a piece of paper tacked up a hundred paces away. She'd never taken a life before, but she knew she was strong enough to do what had to be done. But could she live with herself after? The little voice in the back of her mind kept asking the question, and she didn't know the answer.

The scuffle of feet moving across the pavement proved Shane's theory right. The shooter was changing positions, trying to trap them between the dumpsters and the motel. She'd have to anticipate his moves and catch him off guard. If the shooter made it to his destination they'd never make it out alive.

She concentrated on breathing and listening for the telltale signs of movement—the whisper of clothing as it brushed against a car, the scrape of shoes, a spent magazine falling to the ground and a new one being loaded. She glanced at Shane and saw his eyes were steady on hers. He gave her a nod of approval.

Rachel looked between the two dumpsters and caught a glimpse of a man. He was soft around the jowls and hard around the middle. Built like a boxer, with a nose to match. She didn't recognize him, but she recognized the type. He was dressed in a drab suit with a hat pulled low over his brow. He carried his weapon like he'd had lots of practice using it and had enjoyed every minute. There was no doubt in her mind he worked for Angelo Valentine.

She took aim and waited until he moved closer, but he sensed her movement and raised his gun in her direction. She had only a split second to think before she fired. His gun discharged only a moment after hers, but his aim wasn't true. The .22 stayed steady in her hand as she watched the man fall to the ground. It had been a direct hit, and she knew he wouldn't be getting up again.

Jimmy Grabbaldi should have taken retirement sooner.

When the shooting stopped, the man from the office stuck his head out the door.

"I've called the police," he yelled. "You folks had better pay for destruction of private property." He slammed the door, slid the locks into place, and pulled the shades. Apparently Jake had some standards after all.

The sirens grew closer and Rachel looked down at Shane. He was losing consciousness, though the bleeding from his shoulder had turned sluggish.

"I'll be right back," she told Shane and ran out into the parking lot. She found exactly what she was looking for in the last row of the lot. A beige Volvo still had the keys dangling from the ignition. The shooter's car. She got in, turned the key and it purred to life. She drove to where Shane was lying and loaded him into the back seat.

"We've got to get you to a hospital. You've lost too much blood," she said.

"No, no hospital."

"Don't be ridiculous, Shane. You can't go on like this and last I checked I'm not a nurse. You need stitches and a brain scan, neither of which I can provide."

"No hospital," he said again. "I've had worse than this."

His wallet landed in her lap, but she didn't take her eyes off the road. She wasn't going to argue with a man who obviously had no common sense.

"There's a number in my wallet. Find one of the burner phones and call Wildcat. Tell him what's happened and that we need an immediate safe house. I can rest there for a couple of days until I'm back on my feet."

"Shane," Rachel said, shaking her head.

"I'm trusting you to do as I ask, Rachel. The minute we step foot inside a hospital you'll have Angelo's men all over you. I'd rather die than let that happen. Promise me you'll do as I ask."

She looked at Shane in the rearview mirror. His face was pinched with pain and he was fighting to stay conscious until she agreed to his plan. She'd never forgive herself if anything happened to him, but she found herself nodding in agreement.

"I promise," she said and watched as his eyes closed and his body went slack.

Rachel waited until she was over the Missouri state line before she stopped for gas and to use the burner phone. They'd been on the run for more than an hour without incident, but she was cautious as she pulled into a gas station in a town called Joplin. Shane was still passed out in the back seat, but his breathing was nice and steady.

She circled the block just to make sure no one was following and then turned into an Exxon station. She pulled in next to the gas pump and filled up, and then she took the scrap of paper that held Wildcat's number out of Shane's wallet. It was impossible not to notice the picture of the pretty brunette behind the thin plastic protector.

Maggie Quincy had been killed in the prime of her life. She'd been a beautiful young woman with intelligent brown eyes and a stubborn chin. Rachel flipped through the other pictures. Most were of Maggie by herself, but there were a couple with both Shane and Maggie. It was obvious from the way they looked at each other that they'd been very much in love. It was ridiculous for her to think he could ever feel that strongly for anyone ever again. He'd had something very special, and part of her believed a love like that could only come along once in a lifetime.

Rachel didn't know anything about the man she was calling or what to expect, but she called him anyway and hoped Shane knew what he was doing. The phone rang several times and she was about to hang up when a man finally answered.

"This better be important," the man said.

"Is this Jones Daugherty? Wildcat?" she asked.

"Maybe. Who the hell is this?"

This wasn't the voice of the man she'd pictured in her mind. She'd pictured Jones Daugherty as a respectable FBI agent—soft spoken, with an obvious need to help others and search for justice. Why else do the kind of work he did? No, this guy sounded like he chewed nails regularly and stomped innocent victims into the ground just for laughs.

"This is Rachel Valentine. Shane told me to call you."

"What's wrong?"

"He's been shot in the shoulder and I think he's got a concussion. He refuses to go to a hospital, and he told me to tell you we need a safe house that's close by. Idiot. He thinks he's Superman."

Wildcat laughed at that. "Don't we all. He's suffered from worse than a puny gunshot to the shoulder, and his head's as hard as a rock. I'd be surprised if he didn't crack the pavement. If he tells you he doesn't need a hospital then he doesn't."

"I'm getting a little tired of the testosterone," she said. "Heaven forbid any of you macho men do the sensible thing."

"Honey, if you'd lived through some of the things that we have you'd do your best to never do another sensible thing again. Where are you?"

Rachel sighed out a frustrated breath and gave up on trying to talk sense into him. "A gas station in Joplin. I'm on a burner."

"Give me the number and let me call you back in a few minutes. I don't know what we have available in that area."

Rachel gave him the number and he immediately hung up. She was beginning to think Jones Daugherty worked in internal affairs because he lacked people skills.

The phone rang exactly five minutes later and he gave her directions to a place less than half an hour away and the alarm code so they could get in.

"I'm still working on a few other things Ace asked for, but I'll head in your direction after I leave the office this afternoon. It'll be late tonight before I'm able to get there, so don't let him die. He still owes me ninety-seven dollars from a poker game a couple of years ago. Keep the doors locked and don't go outside for anything. And stay alert."

Jones hung up without giving her a chance to say thank you. Rachel stared at the phone a few seconds and went back to the car. She grabbed some cash out of Shane's wallet, locked the doors, and pocketed the key. There was no way she'd make it to the place Wildcat had told her of without a map.

The inside of the service station wasn't very busy. Only a few customers stood in line and a few others milled around the store. Music played on a radio in the background and people talked softly.

She grabbed a map, a few candy bars, a bag of peanuts, a Coke for her and a bottle of water for Shane. She found a few medical supplies on the opposite aisle and picked up the items she thought Shane would need. It looked like she was going to spend the next couple of days playing Florence Nightingale.

She got in the back of the line and tapped her foot impatiently, every second seeming like a millennium. The teenager in front of her was paying for his gas in pocket change, and if she'd had the extra cash she would have paid for him. When the kid finally left and it was her turn at the counter, she laid down her items and hoped she hadn't forgotten anything. She had no idea what kind of supplies would be in the safe house—whether the refrigerator would be stocked or if there'd be sheets on the bed. Beds, she corrected. She couldn't spend another night sharing a bed with Shane. It was torture at its finest.

The radio announcer picked that moment to issue an urgent bulletin.

"This information has just been released in a joint statement by the Tulsa Police Department and the FBI. The body of an unidentified man was discovered this morning with a gunshot to the head. An eyewitness claims two people are responsible for the death, and that they drove away in a tan sedan heading northwest. The witness believes one of the suspects was severely injured in the shootout, and the police corroborated the theory as they found blood other than the victim's at the scene. The police have issued arrest warrants for Shane Quincy of Louisiana and Rachel Valentine of Illinois, and both are to be considered armed and dangerous. The FBI believes these two individuals are also responsible for the death of Galen Marsh, a high-profile attorney who once unsuccessfully tried to put Dominic Valentine behind bars."

Rachel kept her head down, not making eye contact with the man behind the counter, but she noticed he paused to look at her as he began to check out the rolls of gauze and first aid items. She'd never stopped to think that she was wearing Shane's blood on her shirt. Her appearance hadn't occurred to her once since she'd left Tulsa, and now she'd as good as advertised that she was a wanted criminal to a room full of people.

The radio announcer went on to explain her connection with the Valentine "mob family," and how she'd been thought to have disappeared with her father eight months before. No one knew for sure if they'd gone underground or if they were dead.

Rachel counted out money and was relieved to see she had just enough. She grabbed the bag off the counter, mumbled a hurried, "Thank you," and went out the door, feeling like everyone in the store had been staring at her. And when she glanced behind her it was obvious they had been.

She kept her head down on the way back to the car but used her peripheral vision to look and see if anyone in the parking lot was overly interested in her. The Volvo came into sight, and she hit the remote to unlock the doors, sliding into the seat and then immediately locking them again.

Shane was still asleep in the back seat, but he was roused awake as she started the engine.

"Did you call him?" he asked groggily.

"Yeah." Rachel looked both ways and then sped out of the parking lot. She had a feeling their good fortune was quickly running out.

"Where are we headed?" Shane asked.

"To a little town called Alba. Your friend will meet us there tonight to make sure you're still alive. Don't move around back there. I don't want you to reopen the wound on your shoulder," she said, navigating the turns. "How are you feeling?"

"Hell of a headache. Otherwise, I've felt worse."

Rachel dug around in the sack of supplies she'd just bought and handed him a bottle of Tylenol and the water. He swallowed three pills and drank half the water and then poured the rest over his shoulder so he could see the damage.

"It's not as bad as it looks," he said. "It's a clean wound."

"I bought some supplies back at the gas station and found out some interesting news."

"Yeah?" Shane asked. "Like what?"

"Like we have warrants out for our arrest. It was on the radio."

"I'm sure the cops down in New Orleans are getting a kick out of that information. I'll be hearing jokes for months when this is over."

"I'm glad you can stay focused on the important things," she said, rolling her eyes.

They were headed down Highway 43 past the Joplin Airport when a black sedan pulled out in front of them.

Chapter Nine

Rachel hit the brakes and swerved. The tires squealed and the smell of burned rubber filled the air. She heard Shane mumble a curse as he was jarred against the car door, and she braced herself for impact as the guardrail loomed before them. The crunch of metal was grating as the front of the Volvo glanced off the rail. There was a shatter of glass and then all was silent.

Her breathing was heavy and her hands gripped the wheel in a white-knuckled grasp. She wasn't hurt, and the crash hadn't been bad enough to deploy the airbags. She was just shocked.

"Are you okay?" she asked Shane.

"Dandy." Shane moved into a sitting position so he could see the other vehicle.

The black sedan was pulled across the road so they were blocked in, and the windows were tinted so the inside couldn't be seen. Cars honked as they drove around the black sedan and traffic was beginning to pile up behind them.

"We need to get out of here," Shane said urgently.

"Where am I supposed to go? We're blocked in."

"I don't know, but the guy in front of us has reinforcements coming."

Rachel looked out the back window and saw a sedan identical to the one parked in front of them driving up the shoulder of the road and parking behind them.

"What should I do?" she asked.

Two doors opened from the black sedan and legs emerged. The driver was tall and dressed in black. His head was shaved and dark glasses covered his eyes. His topcoat was unbuttoned and he held a gun down at his side. The man from the passenger side was shorter and stockier but dressed nearly the same, including the gun.

"Floor it," Shane yelled.

"Oh, man," Rachel said, putting the car in reverse and moving away from the guardrail with a squeal of tires. "Hold on tight." She put the car in drive and punched the gas pedal to the floor. The tires spun and smoke rose from the pavement, but then the car took off like a shot. She headed straight for the black sedan and said every prayer she knew as the men raised their guns.

Both men dived out of the way as the Volvo hit the side end of the car. There was a crunch of fiberglass and the black sedan was pushed aside. Rachel jerked against her seat belt and hit her head on the driver's side window. A gunshot shattered the back window and she ducked low in her seat.

"Take the off-ramp to the airport. The guys in the other car are getting closer," Shane said and Rachel turned the wheel just in time to take the exit.

Rachel weaved through traffic with the pedal mashed to the floor, but the guys following them still gained ground. "What are you doing?" she asked as Shane folded down the back seat so he could reach into the trunk.

"I'm seeing if the previous owner of this car had anything that might be useful in a situation like this one."

Rachel felt like an idiot. She'd never thought to check the trunk when they'd been stopped at the gas station.

"And bingo," Shane said.

Rachel kept one eye on the road and the other on Shane as he pulled a hard-shell black suitcase out of the trunk and opened the lid. He had a rifle put together almost before she could blink.

"Umm, Shane," she said nervously, looking at what was coming up.

"A little busy right now, sugar. Just keep driving."

"Tollbooth," she said softly.

"What?"

"There's a freaking tollbooth in front of us!" she screamed. "And I'm a little short on change right now."

"You'll just have to wing it. Try to keep the car in a straight line. No sudden movements," he ordered.

Rachel was beginning to miss the concussed Shane who couldn't open his mouth. She growled low in her throat and kept the pedal pressed to the floor. The booths were all manned and the gates were slowly letting people through the line. She found a lane with no cars and did as Shane said.

He grunted as he lifted the rifle so it was propped on the back of the seat. His shoulder was bleeding again, and she knew he had to be in a tremendous amount of pain. If they got out of this alive, she swore she'd play Florence Nightingale without any complaints.

"What are you waiting for?" she asked as the gate got closer. Panic and fear rose in her throat, but she kept driving, both hands steady on the wheel. A man stuck his head out of the tollbooth and waved his arms, gesturing for her to slow down.

But when she didn't comply he opened the back door of the booth and ran away. Rachel didn't blame him. She wanted to run away too.

She squeezed her eyes shut at the last second and they crashed through the gate. Cars swerved and horns blared, but she kept the car moving forward in a straight line. The black car was through the gate seconds behind them. She heard two pops from the rifle in Shane's hands and the squeal of brakes. The black car's tires blew out and it flipped into the air, rolling across four lanes of traffic.

Rachel let out the breath she'd been holding.

"Right there," Shane said, pointing to a parking garage. "That's long-term parking. We'll make a quick car switch and get out of here. We've got to get back to the main road before they get smart enough to close all the airport exits. It'll take them at least another ten minutes to get things organized. The police don't have the authority to shut down the airport. It has to go through federal channels."

Rachel pulled into the long-term parking lot and into the first empty spot she came across.

"Stop!" she said as Shane tried to get out of the car by himself. "You're bleeding too much. Let me help you get out."

"I can take care of myself," he said. "Pop the trunk and get whatever's in there while I find us a car."

Rachel blew out a breath of frustration and did as he said. There'd be plenty of time to argue with the stubborn man later. She gathered a couple of duffle bags that were in the trunk and stood by, silently arguing with herself, as Shane struggled to stand upright and pick the lock on an old Honda Civic.

The car door opened and Shane slid behind the wheel, his hands clumsy as he took the plastic off the underside of the wheel and stripped the wires. Rachel threw the bags in the back seat and waited outside the car until she heard the purr of the engine.

"Don't even think about driving," she said. "You wouldn't make it down the block."

Shane scooted across to the passenger side and leaned his head back against the seat. He closed his eyes for a second and caught his breath. Sweat beaded on his brow and his hair was damp with perspiration. His skin was pale and his breathing labored.

Rachel pulled the stolen car back out to the main road and was glad to see Shane had been right about the authorities not being organized enough to shut down the airport in a timely manner. Too much red tape. God bless it.

"Give me the map," Shane said. "I'll see if I can find a back road to get us to the safe house. The less visible we are the better."

Shane navigated her down one-lane dirt roads and what looked like cow pastures. She never would have found her way to the little town without his help. It was barely a speck on the map with a total population of less than five hundred.

"There it is. County Lane 245," Shane said, pointing out the window to a wheat field.

"There what is?" Rachel asked. "There's nothing out there."

"Look at the fence and tell me there's nothing out there."

Rachel looked at the expensive iron fence that was weaved with barbed wire and thought Shane might have a point. She pulled the car onto a dirt drive and stopped at the gate. An electric keypad sat off to one side, so she rolled down her window and entered the code Jones had given her, keeping her fingers crossed that it worked and a team of FBI agents wasn't about to swoop down on them.

The gate opened slowly in front of her and she drove the car through. She needed a shower, a hot meal, and a big glass of wine. Rachel looked over at Shane and saw he was slumped forward, only his seat belt keeping him upright. She reached over and touched his forehead. He was burning with fever and his face was flushed. The other things could wait. Shane was her first priority. If only she could find the stupid house.

Rachel drove down the dirt path for more than

a mile before seeing anything other than waist-high grass and wheat. A big red barn came into view, and it looked to be in bad shape. Windows were broken and wood had rotted away, leaving holes large enough for a horse to walk through. But the dirt road continued around the side of the barn, so she kept following it and ended up inside the barn itself.

She was in a garage of some sort and there was a perfectly sturdy-looking wall right in front of her. There was a thick metal door with no doorknob and a keypad similar to the one at the front gate next to it. It looked like the old barn was just a cover for the real safe house. She put the car in reverse and pulled out of the garage, turning the car around so she could back it in—just in case they needed to make a quick getaway. She'd learned that little trick early on in her attempts at running away.

She assumed the keypad used the same entry code as the front gate and typed it in. A little green light flashed above the door and she heard the snick of a lock. She pushed open the door, unsure of what she'd find waiting for her on the inside, considering what the outside looked like.

It was a small space, but it was clean and there were no holes in the walls. After staying at Jake's otel almost anything would be an upgrade, but this would do nicely. She went back to the car and tried to wake Shane. He mumbled something incoherent under his breath but didn't open his eyes.

"Come on, tough guy. I need your help here," she said as she moved under his arm and tried to pull him out of the car. The man was solid muscle and had a good hundred pounds on her.

"I knew you wouldn't be able to resist me," he said, nuzzling her neck.

"Yeah, you're a real catch right now."

He stumbled against her as she walked him into the house and closed the metal door with her foot. She led him into one of the two bedrooms and laid him down gently on the bed. He was burning with fever and hot to the touch. She had to get him out of his clothes and cool him down. And then she had to figure out what to do about the wound in his shoulder.

Rachel turned to get the bag of supplies out of the car, but a strong grip around her wrist stopped her in her tracks. Shane pulled her down so she was sprawled on top of him.

"Don't leave," he said. "It's too dangerous."

His grip was powerful, bruising, and it amazed her how much strength he had even in the condition he was in.

She tried to soothe him as best she could. He was getting agitated and tossing and turning on the bed, no doubt because of the fever.

"I'm not leaving. I just need to get a few things to make you feel better."

"Promise me," he said, increasing his grip till she yelped at the sting. "Everyone I love is always leaving me. Can't take it anymore. Hurts too bad."

Rachel assured herself that he didn't know what was saying, but it was still a nice feeling for him to believe he loved her. "I promise I won't leave you." She bent her head and kissed him softly on the cheek.

Rachel ran and got the bags out of the car and dropped them in the dining room. Wildcat's instructions rang in her head, and after the day they'd just had she didn't want to take any chances, so she double-checked the door locks and looked around the house for an alternate way to enter. Or exit.

The place was very plain, laid out like a small two-bedroom apartment. The floor and walls were beige, as were the countertops and bathroom fixtures. She didn't find any other doors or windows in the house. There was only one way in and one way out as far as she could see, and claustrophobia wound its way around her. Having an alternate route of escape had been a habit since she'd first disappeared, and she hated the feeling of being trapped.

Rachel rifled through the drawers and cabinets until she found the things she needed for Shane—

scissors and plenty of towels and rags. She carried the bags of supplies into the bedroom along with a large bowl of water. It was time to get down to business and get Shane back on his feet. She could freely admit now that she needed him to help her get out of this mess alive.

"Okay," she said, preparing herself. "We've got to get those clothes off." She held the scissors in her hand and looked nervously at the man lying before her. "Suck it up, Rachel. You've seen a naked man before." But her subconscious was telling her she'd never seen a naked man like Shane Quincy before. And she knew her subconscious was right.

Rachel cut away his shirt and winced as she pulled it away from the wound at his shoulder. The blood had caused the shirt to stick to the skin and she had to soak it with water before it would come free. She pulled off his socks and shoes and tackled the button of his jeans. His chest and stomach were hard with muscle and a fine sprinkling of dark hair covered his chest and trailed its way down below the waistband of his jeans. Rachel chewed on her lip nervously and tugged at the denim at his hips. And when she finally pulled them off and got a good look at Shane Quincy in all his glory, she was pretty sure he wasn't the only one who was burning with fever.

"Maggie," he called out, thrashing around on the bed, his sweat-soaked body already dampening the sheets. "Maggie!" His demands for his dead wife grew stronger the higher his fever went, and Rachel felt tears sting her eyes at his obvious pain.

"Ssh, it'll be okay," she soothed. "I'm here with you, and nothing bad is going to happen."

"Rachel?" he whispered.

"That's right. It's Rachel." She bathed him with cool water and cleaned the wound at his shoulder. He was right that it wasn't so bad. There was only a small entry and exit wound, and the area didn't seem to be infected. She applied some salve and wrapped it in bandages.

It was the knot on his head that looked bad. A lump the size of an egg protruded into a starburst of color. She'd read somewhere that a person needing to stay awake while they had a concussion was just a myth, but she wasn't sure. She tried to wake him and get him to swallow more painkillers, but he was too out of it.

It was well after dark by the time she'd finished seeing to Shane's comfort. She took a quick shower, heated a bowl of soup, and ate standing over the sink while watching the clock on the wall. It was ten o'clock and Jones Daugherty still hadn't shown up. Was it just a coincidence that the men in the black cars had found them so soon after she'd talked to Wildcat? She couldn't be sure, and she didn't know what Wildcat's absence meant, but the gnawing in her stomach told her it couldn't be good. She was beginning to think Shane needed to think twice about who he could trust.

Rachel checked the door and made sure the code was set before turning off the lights and climbing into bed next to Shane. He was still as death, and Rachel wondered if he'd remember the promise she'd given him to never leave him. She curled up next to him and tried not to think about the day she'd have to break that promise.

Chapter Ten

Two days and nights passed, and there was still no change in Shane's condition.

Rachel's nerves strung tighter the longer time went on and no word came from Jones Daugherty. She found herself jumping at every creak and shadow, and the safe house was starting to feel like a prison instead of a haven. The duffle bags that had belonged to the shooter in Tulsa were full of guns and cash, and she made sure each weapon was loaded and put in a spot she could reach easily.

The wound in Shane's shoulder was healing nicely, but the fever hadn't gone away. He woke in fits and starts, and his body was restless on the bed. His speech was jumbled and incomprehensible, except for the times he'd called out for Maggie. It was Maggie he saw in his fevered state, and he'd begged her forgiveness repeatedly. Rachel tried not to let the slip hurt her, but it had. Because she could never be the woman he really wanted.

His nightmares hadn't stopped just because of his injuries, but now he was trapped in them, caught somewhere between the past and the present, and the torture only stopped when the final scene had played out. It destroyed her to see his torment over and over again, and she was helpless to stop it.

Rachel did her best to cool his fevered body off with damp rags, but his skin was hot to the touch and seemed to grow hotter as the hours passed. She whispered assurances in his ear as he thrashed about on the bed and held him down when his struggles loosened the bandages over his shoulder. She'd had little luck getting medicine or soup down his throat, but the few times he'd woken she'd cajoled, begged, or forced them down. She went to bed each night feeling as if she'd fought a battle. And lost.

Shane drifted awake slowly, his mind disoriented and his body aching. Something wasn't right, but he couldn't put his finger on what it was exactly. He took stock of his body, cataloguing the stiffness in his shoulder and the nagging headache just behind his eyes. He stretched his sore muscles slowly, and cool sheets shifted around his naked body. And as he moved something soft and warm pressed up against him.

He'd know the feel of her anywhere. The scent of her. She was unique in every way, and he was beginning to get used to the way his body hardened every time she was near. But why was Rachel in bed with him, and where were they? What had they done? And why couldn't he remember?

She was pressed close enough to him so he could feel every curve of her body. He drew her closer and she tangled her legs with his in sleep. Her skin was silky smooth and her hair fell softly over his chest. Her breathing was slow and steady, and he found it sweet the way she snuggled into him, as if she needed him to sleep peacefully.

He wanted her. There was no doubt about that. But he still had his honor, and he knew he could never give her what she deserved. But would it hurt to just kiss her once? To feel the comfort of her embrace?

He could press his advantage. He knew by the way she clung to him that she trusted him, that she felt comfortable with him. And by the way her body moved in her sleep he knew she wanted him. The body was always more honest than the brain.

He shifted, gritting his teeth against the sharp pain in his head at the sudden movement. It wasn't so bad once he gave himself time to adjust. He was just weak. In more ways than one.

Rachel moaned softly in her sleep, and the aches and pains in his body disappeared as his blood ran hot. His lips touched the crook of her neck and then he worked his way up her jaw to her ear.

"Please," she whispered in her sleep. "I need you."

He could stop before things went too far. Maybe if he kept telling himself that he'd eventually start to believe it.

When his lips eventually met hers it was like taking a cool drink of water after being stranded in the desert. A feeling rose up inside him that was familiar but foreign at the same time. It was like coming home after a long trip and being greeted by a stranger who knew all of his favorite things.

Boy, was he in trouble. Because Rachel Valentine was the kind of woman who could make him forget that he'd vowed to go through the rest of his life alone.

He pulled away and dropped his head back on the pillow, moaning as his headache returned. It was less than he deserved.

Rachel opened her eyes but only saw darkness. Her heart thudded in her chest and tears ran down her cheeks. She wasn't sure why other than the fact that kissing Shane had been better than any other physical experience she'd ever had. He made her want things she'd never been able to dream of—a life with a man she loved—a family. The kind of family that went to barbecues and church on Sunday instead of laundering money and fitting people for cement shoes.

He was delirious. He had to have been. There was no other reason to kiss her like that. And the sad thing was she wouldn't have stopped him if he'd pressed for more. He had more integrity in a fever-induced sleep then she did wide awake.

She was angry at herself. And ashamed. And she'd never felt more alone than she did right then. He didn't really want her. It was important for her to remember that. She'd been called Maggie enough in the last two days to feel a bitter jealousy toward a woman she hadn't even known.

The anger at herself was quickly replaced by anger at him and her tears dried quickly. She wasn't a substitute for anyone. She deserved better than that.

She sat up quickly and rolled out of bed, pulling the sheet with her since she was only wearing a loose T-shirt.

"What's wrong?" Shane asked. "Did you hear

something? God, this headache is really getting on my nerves." He felt around on the nightstand until he found the lamp and flipped it on.

She blinked at the brightness of the light and wished she were back in darkness.

"What's wrong?" she asked. "What's wrong! How could you do this to me?"

"Do what? Kiss you?" he asked. "I'd like to remind you that you were kissing me back. Very enthusiastically I might add."

"This isn't a joke," she said. "You took advantage of the situation."

He rolled his eyes and then grabbed his head. "Well, it's not as if I got shot on purpose just so I could have my wicked way with you."

"I was taking care of you, you ungrateful—" She couldn't even finish the sentence she was so angry. "I was asleep," she finally said.

"So was I. And it's not as if you were fighting me off. What's this really about, Rachel?"

"Let me make this as plain as possible. I will not be a substitute for your wife. I'm not her. I never will be, and I wouldn't be if I could. I don't fall into bed with men I've just met. And I won't fill the needs of a man who's been calling me the name of another woman for the last few days. You don't know me, Shane Quincy. You don't know my needs or my desires or the dreams I have. I'm not your wife."

Shane's face grew dark in anger at her words. He rubbed his hands through his hair in frustration and stood up to face her, unmindful of his nakedness.

"I've been in a fever-induced haze for God knows how long, and I don't remember any of it, so if I called you another name I'm sorry. Blame it on the fever. But let me assure you that I know exactly who you are when my lips are on yours. I've kissed you twice and both times you seemed more than happy with the arrangement. I'm not a mind reader. What exactly is it that you want?"

"I want to get out of this mess alive," she said, more calmly than she felt. "And if you'd prefer not to see things through to the end due to our current situation, we can certainly terminate our business arrangement. But if we do go on together, I want you to keep your hands to yourself. I need a man who can only see me. Who can love me. Make a family with me. I've lived in the shadow of my family's name my entire life. I will not live in a shadow in a relationship."

"Understood, sugar," Shane said. "But maybe you should sleep in your own bed from now on just to make sure."

Shane turned around and walked into the bathroom, slamming the door behind him. She heard the shower turn on and went into the other bedroom to put on clothes and get herself together.

It didn't seem to matter what she did or how she tried to protect herself. It looked like Shane Quincy was going to break her heart anyway.

Shane leaned his head against the cold tile of the shower and wished he knew what the hell had just happened. He tried to think back over the last few days, but the hours seemed to run together. He vaguely remembered Rachel always being there when his eyes opened, shoving pills and food down his throat and going back and forth between pleading and arguing with him to get better and wake up.

Well, he was awake now, and all he wanted was to kiss her again. He wanted to make love to her. He wanted to get to know her needs and desires and dreams. But all those things meant forever. And that scared him because he wasn't sure if he believed in forever anymore. He knew better than anyone how temporary, and how fragile, life was.

He had no idea why Rachel would think he was comparing her to Maggie. Maggie was gone. She would always be a part of him, but she was his past. Rachel was his future.

His eyes widened as the realization slammed into him like a Mack truck. He'd known Maggie five minutes before he knew they were supposed to be together. And it had taken even less time to know the same about Rachel. He wanted her to be his future. Convincing her of that might be a little harder.

No wonder she was angry with him. It was obvious she'd already thought through the consequences of how things would be between them if they took their attraction too far. He'd already told her he would never give all of himself to a woman again. And she'd taken the words inspired by his nightmares to heart. He only had himself to blame for saying something so stupid. So hurtful.

The hot water pounded on his sore muscles, and he didn't care about the bandage at his shoulder getting wet or that the water stung the raw knot at his temple. At least he was alive. The amount of pain rioting through his body told him that much. He wanted to feel whole again, and right now he just felt tired and defeated. Some bodyguard he was. He'd spent God knows how long in unconsciousness while his charge had gone unprotected. Anything could have happened to Rachel while he'd been down. And he refused to be responsible for the death of anyone else he loved.

Shane soaped up and rinsed off quickly, the layers of sweat and sickness swirling down the drain along with the despair he felt. He could fix things with Rachel, but they had to get out of their current situation. There was enough to deal with without adding personal feelings to the mix.

He turned off the water and got out on shaky legs. He needed food and something to help the headache he couldn't remember not having. It was time to take back control of the situation. He wrapped a towel loosely around his hips and walked back into the bedroom.

He heard Rachel moving around in the kitchen and decided from the way she was banging pots and pans around that her mood hadn't improved. It was probably best to give them both a little space for the time being. She needed to cool off and he needed to come up with a plan.

The sheets had been stripped off the bed and a washing machine rumbled from somewhere in the house. He found his jeans folded on the dresser. They'd been washed, but holes had been torn in both knees from his fall. A stack of new shirts in several different sizes sat folded in the drawer along with white athletic socks and a package of underwear. He dressed and did nothing more than towel-dry his wet hair, and he gave a cursory thought to shaving when he rubbed his hand across the stubble on his face. The idea was quickly dismissed as the smell of something hot reached his nose.

His system was off and he had no idea what time it was. The clock on the microwave said six, but he wasn't sure if it was a.m. or p.m. Rachel had sandwiches and soup sitting on the table when he came into the room. Her dark hair was pulled back into a knot at the base of her neck and thin wisps of hair had slipped free. Her face was flushed and there were dark circles under her eyes. Obviously he'd given her more than one sleepless night.

"I didn't thank you for taking care of me," he said as he sat at the table. Things were awkward between them, but he tried his best to put her at ease. They had a difficult road ahead of them and they needed to be able to communicate. "I know I'm not usually the easiest patient."

She kept her head down and wouldn't look him in the eye. "You would have done the same for me. I just hope you're not overdoing it too soon."

"I know my limits. I'm feeling better. Just a little stiffness in my shoulder, and I'll have to watch accidentally opening the wound since I wasn't able to get stitches. It might still come to that."

"As long as I don't have to give them to you." She sat down across from him and picked at her food. He'd already inhaled his and was on a second helping. Her brow was furrowed and she shifted in her chair. He could tell she had something important on her mind.

"We need to decide how long we're staying here," she finally said. "I'm beginning to go stir crazy, and I'm anxious to get to Chicago, get the list, and hand it over. I know the way Angelo works, and Galen Marsh's death will be just the beginning if we don't see this through as quickly as possible. I don't like being in limbo like this, out here in the middle of nowhere while innocent people are being slaughtered."

"What did Wildcat say when you talked to him?"

"Your pal Wildcat never bothered to show up." The frustration was palpable in her voice. "There's no phone in this place, and I left the disposable cells in the car. Wildcat gave me explicit instructions not to leave the house, and I've spent two days staring at beige walls. For all I know, Wildcat could be sitting outside with either a group of FBI agents or some of Angelo's men. I'm not too anxious to find out which one."

"If Wildcat didn't show up, it's for a good reason. He wouldn't take the chance of leading anyone to us accidentally."

"If you say so, but you mentioned the last time you talked to him that you were sorry you hadn't kept in contact with him over the last couple of years. Two years is a long time, and people can change."

"Not Wildcat," Shane said, shaking his head. "He's as solid as they come. You've just got to trust me on this one."

"Fine. I guess I don't have any choice, but it

doesn't make me feel very safe to know we're locked in here like prisoners with only one way to escape. What were they thinking putting one metal door and no windows in this place? It's enough to drive a person insane."

Rachel tore her sandwich apart in what he recognized as a nervous gesture. She was scared, and the last days were starting to take their toll. He hadn't stopped to consider what she must be feeling. Most civilians he knew would have reached their breaking point long ago. He'd taken her strength for granted and forgotten that she'd lost a father, her home and most likely her friends. He'd let her ramble on and get everything off her chest, and then he was going to suggest she take a nice long soak in the tub and get a solid eight hours of sleep.

"Of course, they could try to burn us out," she continued. "Though I'd hate to think that they'd try the same old, tired routine. I know Dad always had a fondness for keeping people off guard. It was one of his trademarks."

This was information Shane already knew. The last thing he wanted to get into was a conversation about Dominic Valentine. He rinsed his dishes out in the sink and put them in the drain pan to dry. Rachel continued to sit at the table and stare at her untouched food, so he took the liberty of clearing her plate from in front of her and tidying up.

He knew she wouldn't welcome it, but he needed to touch her. To reassure her that everything would be okay. He walked up behind her and put his hands on the back of her neck, ignoring the way she jumped skittishly at his touch. Then he kneaded the knotted muscles slowly until she all but melted beneath him.

"It wouldn't be very practical for a safe house to have only one route of escape," he said, continuing the massage for a few more minutes. "Come on, I'll show you."

Shane took her hand and held it casually as he led her into the second bedroom. He opened the closet door and moved a wooden shelf out of the way. Behind it was a square, no bigger than a suitcase, with a sliding door. "There's your second doorway," Shane said, sliding it open.

It was dark inside and smelled of earth and disuse. Cobwebs clung to the corners.

"Where does it lead?" she asked.

"I don't know, but it'll open up into a bigger tunnel and go for a couple of miles. It's standard for any FBI safe house. But if you have to use it make sure you take a flashlight." He closed the door and moved the shelf back in place.

Shane went into the small living room and

looked at the arsenal of weapons she had laid out. "Looks like you were prepared for anything."

"I figured I had enough firepower to scare anybody who tried to come through that door," she said. "Of course now that I know about door number two, I think I'll opt to take the coward's way out."

"I've never known anyone who was less of a coward than you," Shane said. He picked up a .9mm Glock and checked the magazine to make sure it was fully loaded. He slipped it in the small of his back and headed to the metal door that led to the outside.

"Wait a minute. Where are you going?" Rachel asked.

"I'm going to take a look around the grounds and make sure we're secure. I want you to stay here."

"Like hell," she said. "I want out of this place. And what if you have a relapse or something while you're out there? The bump on your head looks terrible, not to mention how much blood you lost with the hole in your shoulder. You'll feel pretty stupid if you get out there and pass out."

"I'm fine, sugar. Almost as good as new, but I'm glad to see you're so worried about me."

"I'm worried about me," she said with a scowl. "What if your friend turned you in and the FBI is out there waiting for you? We have warrants out for our arrest."

"Huh. I'd forgotten about that," Shane said. "Make sure you use the second escape route if you hear shots." The color drained from her face and shame washed over him. He was still raw from the words she'd spoken earlier, but that was no excuse. Shane brushed a finger down the side of her cheek, but kept his face void of emotion as she jerked back from his touch.

"There's no one out there, sugar," he reassured her. "I just want to get a lay of the land and see what we're up against. If there is someone out there I'll deal with it. This is what I do. If I'm not back in an hour use the door in the closet and get as far away as you can."

Shane closed the door in the face of a very angry woman. He needed to get away and think things through. Two years was a long time, and he was starting to suspect that Rachel could be right. Jones Daugherty might not be the man he remembered.

Angelo Valentine was enraged.

The servants were still cleaning up the mess from his reaction to the messenger who'd had the unfortunate task of telling Angelo that Jimmy

Grabbaldi was dead. It wasn't the fact Jimmy was dead that bothered Angelo so much. He'd been planning to dispose of Jimmy anyway. It was the fact that Jimmy had failed to kill his nightmare of a niece and the man she'd brought in to help her with family business. Angelo couldn't tolerate failure. Wouldn't tolerate failure. There was incompetence all around him—the men who worked for him were easy come, easy go, but incompetent just the same. If he had to dispose of everyone who'd ever failed him, he'd have a very short payroll. How hard could it be to kill a former interior designer, for God's sake?

Angelo walked into the den and poured himself three fingers of whiskey from the decanter over the fireplace. He was expecting company shortly and preferred to have the meeting in comfort rather than his stuffy office—the stuffy office that had once belonged to his brother. Not to mention his guest might find the current state of the office in bad taste. Blood still soaked the Aubusson rug and brain matter was splattered on the walls. He'd found in the past that members of law enforcement reacted strangely to such things.

The oval mirror over the mantle showed a man distinguished in years—the silver at his temples and the lines of age on his face emphasized as much. He didn't have his brother Dom's charisma or the natural leadership, but he held power just the same. He inspired loyalty in his men through fear like Dom never had. Nice guys never finished first in the mob. And Dom had too much nice in his old age. He'd gotten soft and never quite bounced back from the death of his youngest daughter.

The order of events had worked out exactly as Angelo planned, all the dominoes falling nicely into place. First, take advantage of Dom's weaknesses, meaning kill his wife and daughters, and then destroy Dom. Piece of cake.

Rachel would've already been dead if it hadn't been for Dom's harebrained scheme to turn on his business family and his rivals alike. And so Angelo had to move things around in his timetable and dispose of Dom first. Dom's disappearance and eventual death had been easy to orchestrate—members of rival families had been glad to help out once they'd learned Dom had turned traitor. It had been even easier for the grieving brother to take over the reins of the Valentine empire. Rachel was the only loose end left.

Chimes echoed through the house and his butler opened the door. Two sets of footsteps clipped along the marble tile and there was a light rap on the heavy doors that led into the den. Angelo kept his place standing by the stone hearth—a position of power so he could look down on an underling.

"Enter," he commanded.

His visitor didn't seem impressed by the opulence of the room. And his visitor especially didn't seem impressed by the company.

"Mr. Valentine. You said you wanted to see me." The visitor smiled slightly and took a seat in one of the club chairs facing the fireplace. Angelo didn't know why, but he had the sudden feeling he was no longer the one in control.

"There's a certain place in my organization for overconfidence," Angelo said. "This is not one of those times or places. Everyone's usefulness runs out eventually. It's best you remember that."

The visitor nodded, but the small smile never vanished. Sweat snaked down Angelo's spine and dampened the Italian shirt he wore. He could smell his own fear and wondered if the visitor could as well.

"Tell me what your plans are for my niece. I don't want that list to make it out of the bank vault. Do you understand?"

"Oh, I understand, Mr. Valentine. Now it's time for you to understand that I'm the one calling the shots. I don't want any more screwups, and your men thus far have seemed less than competent."

"And you'd better understand where the money's coming from," Angelo said. "Don't disappoint me. And one more thing. A little change from my earlier orders. I want Rachel brought to me alive. Do what you want with the man and anyone else who gets in your way, but I want Rachel to know what happened to her father before she dies. And I want her to know who's going to end it all."

It was everything Angelo could do not to rub his hands together in anticipation. Rachel had caused him considerable trouble, and it was only fair he paid her back in full. Nobody messed with Angelo Valentine, and the knife he carried in the sheath at his side would guarantee it was the last thing Rachel would ever remember.

"Whatever you want, Mr. Valentine," the visitor said, smirking. "But a kidnapping is going to make my price go up by a hundred thousand."

"Or I could kill you now, and find someone else who is more accommodating," Angelo countered.

"You could certainly try." The visitor got up from the chair and walked away calmly, the small smile never wavering.

Angelo didn't take a breath until the front door closed.

Chapter Eleven

Dawn was just breaking over the horizon when Shane stepped out of the house.

Gravel crunched beneath his feet and he looked over the stolen Honda thoroughly to make sure no one had tampered with it. He grabbed the burner cell phone out of the front seat and a look at the screen told him Wildcat hadn't tried to call. Not good news. He shoved the phone in his back pocket and left the protection of the garage area. If there was going to be a showdown, he wanted to be prepared and take every advantage of the land and any resources at his disposal.

Unfortunately, the land they were stuck on had a whole lot of nothing, and there were no resources that he could see in any direction. The dilapidated barn sat in the middle of acres of six-foot-high wheat. Trees were nonexistent and there were no houses.

Shane figured they'd been lucky up to this point. If Wildcat had turned against them their chances for survival had decreased significantly, and it was a danger to stay in one place too long. His old commander was brilliant at combat tactics, but Shane still held hope that his friend would come through for them in the end. Old habits were hard to break.

Shane had used up more than half of the hour he'd given Rachel as a time gauge. He'd had enough time to think of a plan, but there were a lot of things that could still go wrong. There were too many variables that factored into keeping Rachel safe, and he wasn't afraid to admit he was being overly cautious where she was concerned. Maybe he'd lost his edge since Maggie's death. He'd been stuck behind a desk for two years looking for missing persons and tracking down people who were defrauding their insurance companies.

This was not the time to lose confidence in his abilities now that Rachel's life was on the line.

He was heading back toward the house and Rachel when he felt the vibrations under his feet. A black SUV, windows tinted black and dirt flying from under its tires, came up behind him. Shane had the gun in his hand in an instant and hunkered down in the tall stalks of wheat, training the weapon on whoever was about to get out of the vehicle.

The passenger-side door opened and a pair of denim-clad legs stepped out. The woman was petite and her blond hair grazed just above her shoulders, framing an elfin face. Shane would have thought she looked like a perky high school cheerleader if hadn't been for her eyes. She had cop eyes, intense and assessing as she looked around the area for possible threats. She wore a shoulder holster over a casual white T-shirt and thick-soled Vibram boots under a pair of baggy jeans. He had her pegged for a fed, despite the government license plates on the SUV or the casual clothing.

It was the driver of the SUV who finally pulled Shane's curiosity away from the woman. Jones Daugherty walked around the back of the vehicle and joined his companion. Jones had always been a big man, but he seemed like a giant next to the petite woman, and it looked like he'd been hitting the gym hard over the last couple of years. Other than being a little thicker across the chest, he still looked the same—the same blond hair cropped close to the skull in a military style and the same intricate tattoo that ran from his wrist to his elbow.

But there was definitely one noticeable difference. Shane had never seen Wildcat squeeze a colleague on the rear and whisper a suggestion lewd enough to make the colleague in question blush.

"Come on out, Ace," Wildcat called out. "I know you're out there somewhere. I can feel you staring at me. We need to talk."

Shane wasn't really left with any other options. Wildcat was standing between him and Rachel, and his first priority was keeping her safe. Shane stood up slowly and left his hiding place, keeping his weapon trained on the enemy. The action left a bitter taste in his mouth since it was his closest friend at the other end of the target.

Jones met Shane's steady gaze and glanced at the gun in his hand, laughing a little at the sight. He held his hands up in a sign of surrender. "Don't shoot, Ace. Though I probably shouldn't be worried about you hitting me since you've been playing private eye for the last couple of years. I bet you've lost all your instincts, spying on cheating wives and looking for lost kittens."

"Like hell, I have," Shane said indignantly, wishing he hadn't had the same thought mere minutes before. "Anytime you want to go a round just say the word. Who's your friend?"

"We'll get to that. I figure I should start out by telling you I got trapped in Chicago for a couple of days," Wildcat said. "It's a real mess up there, and I couldn't leave in the middle of it without drawing suspicion my way. People have a tendency to keep an eye on IA men since we're considered the bad guys. And the lady you're pointing the gun at is my fiancée. She's a lot meaner than I am, and she'll get real nasty if you shoot me. I've already been fitted for my tux."

"Special Agent Carrie Layne," she said, nodding in his direction and giving him a smile meant to put him at ease. "I've heard a lot about you. And most of it was fairly entertaining. Maybe you could show me the tattoo you got in Afghanistan some time."

"Geez, Wildcat. You told her about that," Shane said, feeling the heat rush to his cheeks.

"There are no secrets between us. Which means your secrets aren't safe either," Jones said, putting an arm around Carrie's shoulders.

Shane signed and lowered the gun. "Maybe we should go inside and talk about this."

Rachel heard the beeps that signified someone was trying to get through the metal door. She didn't want to take the chance that it wasn't Shane, so she grabbed a sawed-off shotgun from her stash and pointed it at the door.

The door opened and a huge man filled the entryway. He was taller and more muscled than Shane, which wasn't an easy feat, and she figured the man could have passed as a fighter in the UFC. Or maybe even the Incredible Hulk. She pumped the shotgun before he could get a foot over the threshold.

"Whoa, honey," Wildcat said. "Let's not jump to conclusions."

The giant of a man stepped to the side and revealed a tiny blond woman, but Rachel looked over her head to the man behind. She breathed a sigh of relief when she saw Shane rounding up the trio. He seemed unharmed and unconcerned about the strangers who had invaded their sanctuary.

"It's okay, Rachel," Shane said. "I'd like you to meet Jones Daugherty and his fiancée, Special Agent Carrie Layne."

Rachel looked at the man square in the eyes and didn't bother to put down the shotgun. "You're late, Agent Daugherty. Have you come to help us or did you spend the last two days setting up a way to trap us here?"

"Are you always this suspicious?" Wildcat asked and took a seat at the kitchen table.

"You could say I've learned to be cautious over the years," she answered.

"I have to say I'm curious to know the answer as well," Shane said. "Especially after I've gone to all the trouble to assure Rachel that you're the most trustworthy friend I have. Now would be a hell of a time to be wrong about that."

"I assure you, Shane, that Jones has had nothing but your best interests at heart since you called him," Carrie said defensively.

"Put the gun away, Rachel," Shane said as he nodded to the woman his best friend had chosen to spend the rest of his life with. "Let's all sit down and talk this out."

Rachel put down the shotgun and took the chair next to Shane. He lounged like he hadn't a care in the world, and she tried to emulate him. The lack of sleep over the past couple of days was beginning to catch up with her, and she found all she wanted to do was climb back into bed.

"I brought the files on the agents you asked for," Jones began and handed over a folder at least three inches thick of papers.

Rachel gave Shane a curious look and waited for him to explain.

"We've already determined that someone in the FBI has been feeding information to Angelo," Shane said. "And more than likely that same agent is responsible for your father's disappearance and the murder of Agent Culver, since only an inside person would know when and where Culver and Dom were meeting. I want you to look through the files of these agents and see if anyone looks familiar to you."

He handed her the file and she flipped back the blue cover with the confidential seal stamped across it. "This could take a while. I had no idea so many agents had worked on trying to catch my father or any of his men."

"These agents are from all over the country," Shane said. "Not just Chicago. Your father had interests in several states."

Rachel began flipping through the pages and Shane turned his attention toward Agent Layne. "How do you fit in here?" he asked. "Are you IA like Jones or do you have a personal interest in the Valentine case?"

"I've never been assigned to any of the Valentine task forces directly," Carrie said. "I work in the Violent Crimes Unit, so sometimes my cases overlap with the guys in Organized Crime."

"Not many agents would be willing to risk their career for people they've never met."

"I'm not like a lot of agents," she said. "If Jones asks for my help, I'm willing to give it because I trust him. He had to stay in Chicago on an assignment and he needed someone to stock this house with food and extra clothing. I was glad to do whatever I could to help, despite it going against director's orders. Sometimes the results outweigh the consequences."

Carrie's eyes were passionate and her Kewpie doll mouth was pressed in a serious line. Shane could tell she meant every word she said and was loyal to Jones. That's all he could ask for his friend.

"You picked a good one," Shane said to Wildcat. "Though how you got her to fall in love with you is a mystery."

"What can I say? I have charm to spare," Wildcat said with a shrug. "Maybe I can loan you some. You're not looking your best right now."

"I've been shot and lying in bed unconscious for two days. How else am I supposed to look?" Shane turned his attention to Rachel to get her support, but her attention was riveted on the file in front of her.

Shane cursed viciously when he saw the picture of himself in her shaking hands. It was his old FBI photo and the pages attached to it described his job on the Valentine task force. Plain and simple, he'd been the one asked to steady the crosshairs on Rachel's father and pull the trigger if necessary. He thanked God it hadn't been necessary.

"What is this?" Rachel asked.

Wildcat winced and Carrie looked on with sympathy at the both of them. Shane kept his expression blank and wondered how to begin. He might as well get it over with, he thought. She wasn't going to like the outcome either way.

"When I first joined the Hostage and Rescue Unit I was given your father as a target," Shane said, his throat suddenly dry. "In fact he was my very first target. It was a hell of an assignment for someone as new as me to the job."

He remembered the congratulatory slaps on the back and looks of envy from some of his other co-workers. It had made him feel like a king at the time, but now it made him feel like the lowest form of life. His military record had been undisputable, which was why the director had passed the file his way.

Shane got up from the table and went to find the makings for coffee. The silence behind him was deafening as he poured dark grounds into the filter and added water. He tried to find his words carefully, but they stuck in his throat. There could be no more secrets between them if he wanted the chance to have a future with Rachel.

Distracted, Shane left the coffee on the counter and returned to his seat next her. "I wasn't pulled onto the team to assassinate your father. A sniper is not an assassin. That's an important distinction for all of us, and being called to take out a target was never something my unit handled lightly. At the FBI, snipers were called in as a last measure to protect something or someone in imminent danger.

"Intelligence found information that your father had copies of some very important documents from Homeland Security and the military. Documents involving weapons. Intelligence also told us that Dom had set up a meeting with Lex

Torrino out in New Jersey to sell the information for several million dollars. It was common knowledge that Lex had ties to terrorist groups, so it was a matter of national security that he never get his hands on those documents. I was set up as a precautionary measure in case the documents were in jeopardy of disappearing. My instructions were to take out both targets if it looked like the briefcase was going to be part of a switch or if Lex got too greedy.

"Dom went to meet Lex in a very public train station at rush hour with the briefcase in hand. They each stopped at a kiosk and grabbed a cup of coffee before finding a table. They were getting down to business when an overzealous agent busted in on them before they could make the transaction. Civilians were everywhere and no one could hear orders over the shouts as agents jumped out of their hiding places with guns drawn. I knew it was a blown mission from that moment, but I had to wait for the FBI to officially cancel my contract to kill. It only took them a couple of minutes to get in touch with me. I didn't even stay around to see what happened. My job was done as far as I was concerned. It turned out intelligence had been wrong and your father's briefcase had a bunch of real estate papers inside and Dom was going to sell Lex some property he owned in New Jersey."

Even now Shane knew he'd just been doing his

job and felt no remorse for what he'd always considered an important service for his country. "It was just a job," Shane said. "One of many I was given over the years. Nothing more. Nothing less."

"If it had come down to it," Rachel asked. "Would you have killed him?"

Shane only hesitated for the barest of seconds before he answered.

"Yes."

Rachel pushed back from the table and walked into her bedroom, shutting the door with a finality that scared the hell out of Shane. Would there ever be a point in his life where the mistakes of his past would stop coming back to haunt him?

Shane went back to the coffeepot and poured himself a large mug of the steaming liquid. Every sip tasted bitter on his tongue. He kept his back turned, wishing for things that could never be when Carrie's soft voice interrupted his private thoughts.

"Let me talk to her," she said. "She'll understand you did what you had to once she has time to think about it."

Shane didn't answer her, but he heard Carrie's light knock and the squeak of hinges a few seconds later.

"Hell, Ace," Wildcat said. "This is my fault. I didn't even think about your information being in the file. I just grabbed it from my home office and drove straight here."

"No, it needed to come out. I should have been honest from the start and told her sooner. She might not hate me so much now if I had."

"You love her," Wildcat said, surprised.

Shane took his coffee, tossed Wildcat a bottled water because he knew his friend never touched any kind of caffeine, and settled back across from him. "I don't know. I want her, but what I feel for Rachel, it's not like it was with Maggie."

"I'd worry more if it was," Wildcat commented. "They're different people. And you've changed since Maggie died. I'm not saying that what you felt for Maggie should ever be replaced, but that doesn't mean it's all that's left out there for you either. You're still alive, my friend. It's time you started acting like it."

"The last few days have made me realize that more than ever. I think I'm starting to feel my age."

Wildcat leaned back his head and laughed. "Hell, you're only thirty-six. I'm three years older than you, and I'm in the prime of my life. Maybe you need to take some vitamins."

"Yeah, I'm sure that would help," Shane said sarcastically. "Or it could just be the blood loss."

"If you hadn't been sitting behind a desk

getting soft for two years, that guy in Tulsa never would have gotten a piece of you."

Shane's only response was a rude hand gesture. "What was the business in Chicago that held you up?" Shane asked. "Does it have to do with Angelo Valentine?"

"You could say that," Jones said, rubbing his hand over his face, his exhaustion showing. "This whole thing has been screwed up from the beginning. Angelo's been busy since you and Rachel left New Orleans. Bodies have been washing up from Lake Michigan on an average of one a day."

"Anyone we know?"

"No, but your girlfriend does. Three days ago a tourist noticed Cleopatra Carlisle floating near Navy Pier with the zoom lens of a camera. The body was fairly fresh, and she'd been dead less than a couple of hours. Death was the standard MO used by Angelo himself—throat sliced to the point that the head was barely attached," Jones said, making a slicing motion across his neck with his finger. "The file on Cleo says she was a close friend of Rachel's. They roomed together at Loyola for four years, and Rachel was her maid of honor last Christmas. The husband was away on business at time of death."

"Damn," Shane said, massaging the headache that still pounded behind his eyes. "This is going to be hard on Rachel. She's going to blame herself."

He got up and rummaged through one of the drawers until he found the bottle of Tylenol. So far it hadn't done anything to relieve the pressure, but he was willing to give it another try.

"Well, it gets worse. The day before yesterday an Agent Jackson Cole washed up about a hundred feet from where the first body was found. Same cause of death as the first victim. He was the new agent in charge of the Valentine case. Word through the office was that Cole had an informer on the inside of Angelo's organization. Apparently Angelo's men aren't too happy with the way things are being run, and there've been a few internal struggles. Director Shaw is mainlining Rolaids and hasn't slept in weeks. His agents keep dying and the higher-ups want to know why."

Shane grunted. "Not a good position to be in, for sure. But he's the man in charge, and the leak is in his office, so it's his responsibility. Do you have an idea on the informer in Angelo's organization?"

"Yeah, his name is Sal Lorenzo. He's in the morgue along with Agent Cole, though it took us longer to find all of Lorenzo's body parts. Angelo was sending a message to his other men."

"You said there was another victim who washed up. Who was it?" Shane asked, the feeling in his gut already dreading what Jones was going to tell him.

"Randall Clark III, or Randy as he was known

to his friends," Jones said. "He lived across the hall from Rachel for the last several years. According to my sources, they'd dated for a short time and had been briefly engaged their senior year of college before deciding they made better friends than lovers."

Shane's head was reeling. Rachel had been engaged? And now a man she'd been close to and had maybe even loved was dead. How the hell was he going to break the news to her?

"Are you going to tell Rachel?" Jones asked. "Or I could do it if you think she'd take it better from me."

"No, I'll tell her."

"Will she be all right? You've gotten to know her better than anyone over the last few days. Our file on her tells us pitifully little."

"From what I've gathered her father tried to keep her out of his business as much as possible. She's led a pretty quiet life up until now, but she's one of the strongest people I've ever met. She'll be okay. But once the news has sunken in about her friends she's going to be out for Angelo's blood. She's not one to sit back and let others take care of problems for her."

"Don't let her do anything stupid," Jones said. "The FBI still wants that list, and it is widely known now that she has the last remaining copy. I wouldn't be surprised if Angelo wasn't the only mobster looking for Rachel."

"Great. I don't suppose you have any ideas how to get her to the bank in Chicago and back out alive? I've gone through several scenarios, but the outcome never seems very favorable."

"I've had a few thoughts on the subject but nothing is set in concrete. Carrie and I need to head back this afternoon. She's got meetings later today. If you'll agree, let me talk to a couple of people and see if we can get some extra help. It never hurts to have backup. I'll also see if we can find the bank president and keep him in a safe place for a couple of days until we figure out when we want to go in."

"Do whatever you need to do. Just make sure the people you tell won't give Rachel's head to Angelo on a silver platter. Do you have an estimate of when you'll be back?"

"No, but you'll be safe here for the time being. We've taken this house off the books, and Carrie and I are the only ones who know you're here. You have plenty of food and extra clothes. Just stay put until I come back for you." Jones stood and Shane did the same. "Will you take some advice?" he asked.

Shane smiled and thought back to the days when Jones was his commanding officer. "Since when do you ask if you can give advice?"

"Good point, so listen up. Don't wait too long to tell that woman you love her. From the way things are going I think it's something she might need to hear. And it's something you, my friend, need to say. Maybe it'll be just the thing to make the nightmares go away."

"How the hell do you know about the nightmares?" Shane asked incredulously.

"I work for the FBI. I know everything."

Rachel thought about using the secret exit in the closet and disappearing again. The idea wasn't completely without merit. She could vanish for good this time. Change her hair and get some contacts. She knew who to contact for a passport and new identity, and she had plenty of cash stashed away in a safe place. Maybe she should just leave the country. And keep in touch with no one. Start over completely with a brand-new life.

The knock on the door interrupted her plans of escape and she cursed her indecision. The last thing she wanted to do was talk to anyone.

"Rachel," Carrie said as she came into the room. "Do you want to talk about it?"

"No, I don't think that's a good idea. I think this is something best left alone." Rachel lay down on the bed and stretched out her tired muscles. She could fall asleep so easily. All she had to do was close her eyes and drift away, but Carrie had other plans. Rachel wasn't in the mood to hear the reasons Shane had chosen the career path he had. And having a woman she barely knew try to explain it made her all the more irritable.

"No one can understand how it feels to be a sniper unless you are one," Carrie said. "That's just the truth. I don't know what it's like and Jones doesn't know, even as close as he and Shane are." She paused as if weighing her words carefully. "And you don't know."

"No offense, Carrie, but I'm really not in the mood to hear this right now," Rachel said. She didn't like the combination of pity and understanding she saw in the other woman's eyes. Couldn't she just have some time alone to think without someone coming along and judging her?

"No offense taken," Carrie said. "But I'm going to say what I came to say anyway, and it's up to you whether or not you listen. What Shane did while he was in the military and the FBI was so important. It's a job that's easily overlooked and always underappreciated. The job itself takes a powerful toll on the body and mind, and the stress that comes from it isn't comprehensible to people like you and me. Not everyone can cut it, and the good ones only last so long before they start to burn out.

And believe me, I've read Shane's file. He was very, very good."

"Believe it or not," Rachel said. "I understand that it was his job and he had no control over his assignments. But I can't reconcile what he used to be to how I was raised. I love my father very much, and now that my whole family is gone it makes hearing something like that even harder."

"But Shane's not to blame," Carrie said.

"I don't know who's to blame," Rachel said. "Only that someone should be. Shane is just wired differently. I don't understand him. He has great compassion and a need to protect the innocent or those who are weaker, but he doesn't bat an eye at taking lives when given an order. At least with the way things worked in my family, I always knew where everyone stood. Things are more cut and dried than you might imagine in the mob. We celebrated birthdays and weddings and funerals, and when someone was killed their families were taken care of. Does Shane even care that his victims had wives and children?"

"Jones and Shane have been friends a long time," Carrie said. "And from some of the stories I've heard, I can tell you that I think Shane cares too much. He was loyal to his country and to the other men he worked with. Then his wife died and he was left questioning everything he'd stood for his whole life. Everything he'd always believed in.

You can't blame a man for his past. We all have things we've done that are better left forgotten. It's the future that counts."

"Yeah, well I don't think we have much of a future," Rachel said.

"You've got to be kidding me," Carrie said with genuine surprise. "That man is completely in love with you. I mean over the moon in love. Open your eyes."

"I think you're wrong. We've only known each other a short time, and it's been under high stress."

"Jones said the two of you have been neighbors for months," Carrie said, brushing away her concern. "I bet you each know each other better than you think you do. You can't tell me you never noticed a man like Shane. Maybe paid a little closer attention to when he was home or away. Noticed who he hung out with or what he ordered for takeout."

Rachel felt the heat rise to her cheeks. "He's the kind of man who's hard not to notice. But that's a long way from love. We all think we know what love is. You and Jones think you're in love. But real love comes after the commitment. Real love develops over time. It's hold one another when you cry through a disappointment or the death of a loved one. It's worrying about careers and life choices that will affect the both of you. It's lying next to them on the cold bathroom floor because they're sick and you don't want to leave them alone. Real love is never in an instant. It's grown. And Shane has already had that with someone. I've already come to terms with him never being able to have that kind of life with me. He's still in love with his wife, and he still blames himself for her death. How can I compete with a ghost?"

"Wow," Carrie said, clearing her throat of emotion. "It sounds to me like you know him better than you think you do. And that the love is already starting to grow. How many days did you lie next to him and take care of him? He owes you his life. And from what I understand, Shane has been nothing more than a machine the last two years, not caring whether he lived or died. He's just been one job after the next, cutting himself off from anyone who cared about him. But the man I just saw in the kitchen didn't look like a machine to me. The way he looked at you was all man. All I'm saying is maybe don't give up on him too soon."

Rachel ran her fingers through her hair and massaged the back of her neck to relieve the tension. She'd never made excuses for her family. She couldn't control whom she'd been born to. She couldn't stop the actions of her father or anyone else. Her mother had drummed into her at an early age that she was to look straight ahead and focus on her own life and goals. To not pay attention to the media or the whisperings of the people around her.

She'd gotten used to bodyguards and armed foot soldiers throughout her childhood and into college. And she'd always known the danger that went along with having the name Valentine. It wasn't uncommon for family members to turn up dead or to end up in prison. It was just part of life. Maybe not a normal life, but it was her life.

But she realized as she'd forged her own path and ignored the messy parts of life that it had been a long time since she'd held on to hope. It was one thing to live your life, day to day and year to year, just breathing and going through the motions. It was another thing to see the ember of hope flicker to life that reminded her she'd once dreamed of having a family and living set apart from the notoriety of her family. And when she'd met Shane, that hope had spurred to life. She could see them living a life together that had nothing to do with their pasts.

Rachel got up from the bed and gave Carrie a light hug. "I appreciate you following me in here. I guess I did need to talk about it. I hadn't realized how long I've lived with fear. I love my father, but I can't help but be angry at the life he chose. I remember being afraid as a child, seeing men with guns or having them surround us and rush us all into a building. I hadn't realized I'd become numb to it until my mother was killed."

"It's okay to love your father and hate what he

did," Carrie said. "It wasn't fair to put you in that position as a child. Or to watch those you love die."

Rachel nodded. "And then my sister was killed and the grief was so much I couldn't feel my heart beat. Maybe I've been a machine too over the last couple of years, just functioning enough to get by. Because if I just function I don't think about the fear. I've never been scared to die. I haven't really thought much about it. But I don't want to lose anyone else I care about, and I care about Shane. It's strange to feel like you've known someone your whole life when you've just met."

"Yeah, well, Jones and I met during a very heated and high-profile serial killer case. We had the guy hunted down within the first forty-eight hours and we were naked and sweaty by the forty-ninth. We were engaged by the seventy-two-hour mark. When you know, you know. Time is relative."

Rachel laughed at her confidence. "Maybe. We'll see."

"I wanted to tell you we're going to have to leave you soon," Carrie said. "I've got a meeting with my unit later this afternoon that I can't miss, but we'll be back. I'm sure Jones and Shane have thought of a plan during their male bonding time out there."

There was a knock at the door and Jones stuck his head in. "Y'all good here?" he asked.

"Yeah," Carrie said. "I think so."

Rachel nodded. "I'm good. Thank you both for your help. Shane's lucky to have friends like you."

"I won't argue with that," Jones said, winking. "We've got to get going. Duty calls."

Shane and Jones walked the perimeter and made sure they were clear to leave, while Carrie stayed with her locked inside. After they'd gone, she and Shane were left alone once again. The silence between them lay heavy, and Rachel wasn't sure what she should do next. She twisted her fingers together and finally brought her gaze to Shane's. He stared at her with a mixture of emotions she couldn't interpret. Emotions she didn't want to interpret.

"We need to talk," he said.

She nodded her head silently and dreaded whatever was to come.

Chapter Twelve

"What's wrong?" Rachel asked.

"Maybe we should sit down first," Shane said, reaching for her hand so he could lead her to the small couch in the living room.

"I'm not a child," she said. "Whatever it is, I can take it."

Shane didn't know where to begin. It seemed like ever since he'd first crossed Rachel's path he'd brought her nothing but heartache and worry.

"Is it my father? Did they find his body?" she finally asked, her voice soft.

Despite her protests he was able to pull her down on the sofa next to him, and he put his arm around her, holding her close. The news wouldn't be any easier the longer he waited. It would be best to tell her straight out.

"No," he said. "It's not your father's body that

was found. I'm sorry, Rachel, but it was Cleopatra Carlisle's and Randall Clark's bodies that were discovered. It's already been ruled a mob hit by the FBI because of certain calling cards that were left behind at the scene."

Rachel shook her head in denial and her face paled at the news. And then he watched with admiration as he watched her collect herself. Her voice was stiff and monotone. "Cleo's husband? Has he been told? I'd like to help with the funeral if possible. We were all very...close."

Shane was watching Rachel for any signs that she might be close to an emotional breakdown, but other than being cool to the touch, her feelings were buried somewhere deep inside of her. Grief was a mysterious thing. Everyone went through the process differently. But it was that moment he wondered if she'd ever grieved at all, or if she'd always done what he just watched her do—pull herself together.

"Cleo's husband was away on business, but he's been notified and is now back in Chicago to see to the funeral arrangements," he said. "I'm so sorry, Rachel."

"They were married just last year," she said. "The last time I talked to her she was excited because they'd decided to try and start a family right away. They were very much in love. They were my friends." Her voice cracked on a sob, but she choked it down ruthlessly.

"I'm so sorry, Rachel. I wish…"

"And what about Randy?" she interrupted. "He doesn't have any family left living. His parents died when he was twelve, and he was raised by a grandmother. Do you think the FBI would let me make the arrangements for his mass once we get out of hiding? He was Catholic, and he'd want things to be done properly."

"I'm sure something can be arranged," Shane said. "It will be a few days before his body is released." He didn't bother to remind her that they were wanted and if she showed her face in the light of day she'd end up in jail or worse.

"Good," she said, extricating herself from his hold and wiping her damp hands on her jeans. "I appreciate you telling me the truth. I know it can't have been easy for you." She got up from the couch and he watched her closely. "I think I'm going to lie down for a little while. I haven't slept well the last few nights and I'm exhausted."

If it hadn't been for the fine tremors in her hands as she rose, Shane would have let her go. She was holding on by a very thin thread, and she was going to wait until she was alone to break.

"Rachel," he whispered, taking hold of her hand and pulling her back down.

"No, Shane, just let me go. I need to be alone."

And then her voice broke on a sob and she collapsed into his open arms.

"It's all right, sugar. Just let it all out." He held her tightly and stroked her hair while her anguish washed over him in waves. He whispered words of love and compassion in her ear, but she was too far gone to understand the significance.

"It's my fault. All my fault," she repeated over and over again.

Her tears soaked his shirt and he knew there was nothing he could do to take away the burden of her guilt. She'd realize soon enough that her uncle would have found a way to hurt her, whether she'd kept in touch with her friends or not.

The tears slowed, though her breath stayed ragged. "They're all gone," she said. "I have no one left. My family and friends, all destroyed because of a choice my father made. One decision that altered the course of so many lives."

He wanted to tell her she wasn't alone and that she never would be, but he knew now wasn't the time or place. "Not all choices are easy, Rachel, and there are consequences that each choice brings. You can't fault your father for wanting to do the right thing."

"No, I can't fault him, but I have to place the blame somewhere. On someone. I can't even think of what's left for me. The hurt just runs too deep. I'm numb with it."

Shane knew only too well how personal pain numbed the soul. There was only one remedy. Time. He held her in his arms for what might have been hours. If he could have taken the pain away he gladly would have, but life didn't work that way.

Her breathing changed and he realized she'd fallen asleep in his arms.

"You're not alone," he whispered against her temple. "You have me. And I'm not going anywhere."

She nestled against him and he lifted her in his arms and took her to the bedroom. It was time for him to take care of her.

"How long have I been asleep?" Rachel asked, covering her eyes with her hands. "Why is the light on?"

"So you're a grumpy riser," Shane said. "Good to know for the future. You've been asleep sixteen hours, and your coffee is on the nightstand."

She growled and squinted at him, making him chuckle.

"I would have let you sleep longer, but I figured you needed to use the bathroom and get something in your stomach. We need to be ready to move when Jones gets back."

Rachel grunted and swung her legs out of bed

and headed toward the bathroom without uttering a word. When she came back she picked up the steaming coffee mug and crawled back under the covers.

"How do you know how I like my coffee?" she asked, testing the temperature with her tongue.

"I pay attention to details," he said. "That's kind of my job. I also know you like quick showers in the morning and long baths at night. You overtip delivery guys and you love fried rice and orange chicken—sometimes they deliver to my place by mistake—and you love romantic arias, though you can't sing to save your life. You buy fresh flowers at least once a week and you've got a green thumb. The plants on your balcony attest to that. You're generous with your money. You like to give to the street performers, even when they're not good. And you were kind enough to leave a saucer of milk outside when 2B's cat had kittens in the shrubs."

He watched the color drain from her face and he grabbed her mug, afraid she was going to drop it.

"What?" he asked. "What's wrong?"

"I just realized that I had no idea you'd been watching me that closely and maybe I hadn't been doing as good of a job at hiding as I'd thought."

"I'd say you've been doing a pretty good job," he said. "You've been on the run for months and you're still alive." His lips twitched and he watched her take another sip. "It just so happens that I'm more exceptional than most in the observation game. You caught my notice at first because you looked familiar at first glance. But you kept my notice because you are quite possibly the most beautiful woman I've ever seen."

She scoffed and said, "You barely said hello to me a handful of times in the two months I lived there."

"I would've talked to you eventually," he said and then he grinned. "Especially considering the way you watched me. At some point I would've stood at your door with your mis-delivered Chinese food and talked my way into sharing it with you. I knew the moment I laid eyes on you my days of being alone and detached were numbered."

She was steadier than she had been before she'd fallen asleep, though there were still dark circles under her eyes. He'd lain next to her while she slept, stroking her hair when she cried in her sleep.

"How are you feeling?" he asked.

She stared down blankly at her half-full cup and let out a slow breath. "I'm sad. I'm sad that my friends paid a price they never should've had to pay. You can tell me it's not my fault, but the truth is, they're dead because they knew me. So it is my fault." She held up a hand to stop him from protesting.

"It is my fault," she said, steadily. "And it's

something I'll always have to live with. My family and my friends, all gone because my last name is Valentine. Which makes me angry. And anger is the emotion I need to focus on right now. Angelo needs to pay. He's destroyed too many lives. And I want to be the one to bring him down."

Shane nodded. Anger was something he could understand. Anger could motivate like nothing else could. She would have to live with her guilt, just like he did. And eventually she'd have to forgive herself. Just like he was starting to do.

"Come on," he said. "I'll make you some eggs and bacon. Anger burns a lot of calories." He held the bedroom door open for her, ignoring the temptation of pushing her back toward the bed. Her hair and clothes were rumpled and there was a crease along the side of her cheek. It was inevitable. And he knew it.

"And one more thing," he said, moving past her to get the eggs out of the fridge. "If you're tired of the name Valentine you could always take my name. Rachel Quincy has a nice ring to it."

Chapter Thirteen

The next two days were some of the best of his life. Shane couldn't remember the last time he'd laughed so much. He'd forgotten that feeling of getting to know someone—every detail of their life—and staying up for hours absorbing every piece of information.

He'd also never been so tortured. Spending that much time with Rachel in close quarters had wreaked havoc on his body. He wanted her. And there had been moments in the night, when she was curled in his arms, where they'd let their lips wander and explore. She was as frustrated as he was, which was the only consolation to his torture.

He needed her to know that she was more than just a warm body in a tense situation. Even if it killed him. But when this was over...

"Penny for your thoughts?" Rachel asked,

coming out of the bathroom in the thin shorts and white T-shirt she liked to wear to sleep in.

His mouth dropped open and became dry as dust at the sight of her. He knew what her skin felt like—soft and smooth—but there was strength beneath the softness. His eyes traveled over every inch of her, eventually reaching her full lips, lingering there for a moment before meeting her gaze.

He saw laughter in her eyes. She knew exactly what she was doing to him, and she didn't seem to care.

"Cat got your tongue?" She approached him slowly, her fingers skimming over his chest and down to his stomach.

"You are playing a dangerous game," he said.

"Really?" she asked. "I appreciate your noble intentions. It's very gentlemanly of you. But I'm tired of you being a gentleman."

Shane swallowed hard and held on to her hands so they'd stop roaming. "It's for your own good. When I make love to you I want you to know it's for no other reason than I want to spend the rest of my life with you. Sex is easy. It's everything else that's hard. I don't want anything to cloud the issue when it comes down to you choosing me."

She kissed along his jawline and his body temperature spiked. "You're driving me crazy,

Shane Quincy. It figures I'd fall in love with the only white knight left in the business."

His breath caught in his chest. "You love me?" he asked, seeking the truth in her eyes.

"I have it on good authority that time is relative. I feel like I've known you forever. And I trust you more than I've ever trusted anyone. That's saying a lot."

Shane felt the tremulous hold he'd kept on himself start to crack and he took her mouth in a kiss meant to devour, a kiss meant to let her know how much he loved her.

He'd lost control of the situation. All of his well-laid plans went right out the window at her touch. Her nails bit into his back and he realized his shirt had disappeared. The red haze of lust flashed behind his closed lids as his lips explored her. He was past the point of no return, and he resigned himself to the fact that temptation had gotten the better of him.

He picked her up in his arms and was carrying her to the bed when he heard the series of beeps alerting that someone was entering the front door. Shane dropped her on the bed and reached for his gun on the nightstand. Unmindful of his nakedness, he ran into the living room, thinking only of protecting Rachel and giving her a head start to escape.

"Get dressed and get into the other bedroom,"

he said, his weapon trained on the door. He saw Rachel out of his peripheral vision and swore. She had the sawed-off shotgun in her hands and was crouched low in the bedroom doorway.

"I'm not leaving you here," she insisted.

"Can't you ever listen—"

"Rise and shine, sleepyheads," Jones said, coming through the front door big as life. "We've got a plan and a small window of opportunity to take advantage of it."

Shane let out a breath and rolled his eyes. "Thanks for the warning, Wildcat. You're lucky you're not standing there with a bunch of holes in you."

"Nah, bullets don't scare me. You should know by now I'm as good as Superman." Jones flipped on some lights. "God Almighty, boy. Go put some clothes on. I'm too young to go blind."

"Don't hurry on my account," Carrie called out, causing Rachel to snicker.

Shane blushed and hurried past Rachel to get his clothes, mumbling things best left unsaid under his breath.

"Sorry," Rachel said, lips still quivering with laughter. "We weren't expecting anyone this late. It's the middle of the night. I think."

"That's the point," Carrie said, coming in and making herself at home. "Though it wouldn't have hurt for Jones to give you a bit of a heads-up."

"What fun would that be?" Jones countered.

Rachel went into the kitchen and put on a pot of coffee. Shane practically lived on caffeine, and she poured him a cup just as he came back into the room, fully clothed. She grabbed a bottle of water for herself and the others.

"So what's this about a plan?" Shane asked.

"We've got the bank president locked up in a safe house, and I've got men watching Angelo," Jones said. "The bank president didn't really want to help us out, claiming something about normal banking hours and customer privacy, but he was real helpful once I showed him a few photos of what Angelo is capable of. He's a real prissy little fellow. Won't let anyone call him anything but Mr. Norman, and he insisted we let him dress in his normal suit and tie before taking him. All we need now is Rachel and we'll swing by and pick up Mr. Norman. Then we'll go together to get the list."

"I hope you've got someone you can trust guarding Mr. Norman," Shane said. "I'd hate to get there only to find he's had his throat slashed."

"I think Cutter and Jax would take offense to that," Jones said.

"Cutter and Jax?" Shane asked, surprised. "You called them in to help with this?" A smile split his face before he could help it. If Wildcat had called in his old squadron then things were dire. It meant Jones didn't trust anyone in the FBI.

"Yeah, you could say they owe me a few favors," Jones said. "The whole team came running as soon as I called. Well, almost the whole team. It took everyone a couple of days to rearrange their schedules and get here, but they were more than glad to help out. Civilian life gets boring after a while. Cutter and Jax are keeping a close eye on Mr. Norman, and Merlin and Dixon are keeping an eye on Angelo's activities. I couldn't get ahold of Doc. He's out of the country on assignment."

"He'll be pissed he missed the fun," Shane said.

"There's no rest for the wicked," Jones said. "You guys pack up your stuff and let's get out of here. It's crunch time."

"Already done," Rachel said, holding up the black bag of weapons they had stashed. "I haven't breathed fresh air in almost a week, and I'm itching to do something besides sitting here waiting."

"Put on a sweatshirt," Carrie said from her lounged position on the couch. "It's gotten cold over the last few days, and we're supposed to have rain coming soon."

"Thanks," Rachel said, noticing for the first time that Carrie and Jones were both wearing jackets over their shoulder holsters. Rachel grabbed a dark sweatshirt from the drawer and another for Shane before rejoining the conversation.

"What do you have in mind once Rachel gets

the papers from the vault?" Shane asked. "She's still not safe until they're in the right hands."

Jones laced his fingers across his abdomen and propped one boot up on the coffee table before he answered. "Dominic Valentine's attorney has been in protective custody since Dom went missing with the first set of papers and Agent Culver washed up on shore eight months ago. I'll have Cutter and Jax go pick him up just as soon as we relieve them of their babysitting duties over Mr. Norman. I also have a federal judge lined up to sign search warrants for Angelo's home and businesses."

"What about the other people on the list?" Shane asked. "They're going to be out for blood once the documents are turned over."

Jones sighed and shrugged his shoulders. "Unfortunately, that's something we have less control over. Until the list Dominic put together has been checked out and confirmed, there's nothing we can do. Rachel will need to go into protective custody until everything is sorted out."

"And how long will that take?" Rachel asked.

"Optimistically, it could be as short as a few weeks. Realistically, it's more likely to be a year," Jones answered.

"No way," Rachel said. "I did just fine for the eight months I was on my own without the FBI's help. There's no way I'm going to be trapped in another place like this one for a whole year. I know how to disappear."

"Yeah, except one of Angelo Valentine's men found you anyway," Shane said.

"I'll admit I made mistakes the last time," she said. "But I promise I can disappear so no one can find me if I really wanted to. And that's exactly what I'll do if they try to force me into being held in protective custody."

"Now, Rachel," Jones said.

"Don't bother," Shane said abruptly. "We'll argue about this later. Let's just get out of here and get things done."

The air was brittle with cold, but Rachel inhaled the icy air with relief. The night was black and the moon barely visible through the gathering clouds in the sky. They left the stolen Honda in the garage and piled into Wildcat's big black SUV.

Rachel knew Shane was angry, but it wasn't something that could be helped. It was probably fortunate that reality had interrupted them before things had gotten too out of hand. Shane wanted forever with her, but she couldn't very well ask him to give up the business he'd created and go on the run with her. What kind of life was that to live? She couldn't blame him for being angry. Their choices were limited.

Rain splattered against the windshield as the navigation system on the dash led them back to civilization. It wasn't until they passed a familiar sight that Rachel knew where they were.

"Why are we back in Joplin? I thought we were going to Chicago?" she asked.

"We've got a private flight chartered to get us there tonight. It's a nine-hour drive by car, and I think our sneak attack would lose its effect if we showed up in broad daylight tomorrow," Jones said.

Rachel was obviously too tired to think rationally or she would have realized this already. "How can you keep all this stuff you're doing for us off the FBI radar?" she asked. "Won't you get into trouble?"

"Nah, but I'm calling in a lot of favors. You're lucky so many people owe me," he said with a cocky smile. For some reason Wildcat's confidence reassured Rachel, and she could tell by looking at Shane that he believed in his friend's abilities with equal certainty.

The Joplin airport looked much different now that they weren't being chased by gun-toting maniacs. Wildcat drove the SUV straight onto the tarmac next to a small twin engine plane that was already running and had the stairs let down for passengers to board. It was obviously a company plane of some sort as the logo on the side read NJEnterprises.

They got out of the SUV and into the steady drizzle. A man stuck his head out of the open door, and Rachel got a glimpse of one of the most handsome men she'd ever seen. He was *GQ* cover model material, but when she got closer she could see the scar that marred his left cheek and left him not so perfect.

"Let's move it, people," the man said. "The weather's only going to get worse and the temperature's dropping." His head disappeared back into the cabin.

"As I live and breathe," Shane said, pushing her up the short flight of steps and into the threshold of the tiny cabin. "Is that you, Jax?"

"And who the hell else would be flying you around in the middle of the night? Just like old times, right, Ace?" And then the man smiled and Rachel was caught momentarily speechless. He was a lethal weapon, and from the wink and slow appraisal he gave her she was willing to bet he knew it.

Shane pulled her close and bared his teeth in a possessive gesture that had her raising an eyebrow. "Rachel, I want you to meet Nikolas Jacks. Don't believe anything he tells you. Jax, this is Rachel Valentine, and she's too smart to fall for you. Hands off. Mine."

"It's a pleasure to meet you, Rachel," Jax said, taking her hand and bringing it to his lips. He smiled at Shane's growl.

"The pleasure is mine," Rachel said, extricating

her hand quickly. She didn't like the feel of another man's lips on her. And then she elbowed Shane in the ribs, making him grunt. "And I'm not a toy to pass around on the playground. Stop acting like a Neanderthal."

"Are you going to make us stand in the rain all night, or are we going to get this death trap off the ground?" Jones asked from behind.

"Don't get your panties in a twist, Sarge. Find a seat and get buckled. I'm ready to fly when you are."

"I thought Jax was supposed to be guarding the banker," Shane said to Jones.

"Cutter and I have been babysitting that guy for twenty-four hours," Jax said. "And if Wildcat here hadn't offered me the chance to fly I would have shot the man myself. He's been treating us like his servants, asking for crushed ice instead of cubed and a relish tray. What in the hell is a relish tray? Believe me when I say Mr. Norman is much safer without me there. Cutter is better at that kind of thing anyway."

"What kind of thing?" Shane asked. "Being around other people without wanting to kill them?"

"Basically," Jax said with a shrug. "The human race is just no good."

"I've told you more than once I know the name of a good therapist who will help you get over this aversion to people," Jones said. "Now, both of you get the hell out of my way so I can sit down. Some of us work for a living."

There were a few good-natured shoves between the men as they made their way into the small cabin. There was only enough seating for the four of them, but the chairs were oversized and made of light gray supple leather. Rachel sat in the window seat and Shane sat down next to her, immediately reclining and closing his eyes. The rain outside was hypnotic as it misted over the bright lights on the runway, but she couldn't relax.

"We're cleared for takeoff," Jax said through the speaker. "We'll arrive at Midway in about an hour and a half. I'm sorry to say this is probably going to be a bumpy ride with the weather the way it is. Stay buckled and grab some shut-eye while you can."

That was easy for him to say, Rachel thought. The last thing she wanted was sleep. There were too many doubts, too many worries, wreaking havoc in her brain. She looked over at Carrie and Jones and saw they were already preserving their energy with a nap. And Shane was no better beside her. Wasn't anyone else worried? If the plan didn't work, they could all be dead by morning.

Shane reached over and took her hand and squeezed it gently, telling her without words to relax. His touch did amazing things to her body, and she almost believed everything was going to turn out all right when he was near.

The plane taxied down the runway, and the rain pelted against the windows harder. The plane shook and shuddered as it lifted into the air, defying gravity and taking on the storm around them. The plane dipped and she felt her stomach rise just before it gained altitude again. She squeezed Shane's hand tighter and tried to think positive thoughts. Like maybe crashing and burning in a plane the size of a tin can was much more preferable to being tortured to death by her Uncle Angelo.

Then again, maybe not.

The plane shuddered once more and the engines went silent just before the lights went off inside the cabin.

Chapter Fourteen

Shane scowled at Jax as he threw an arm around Rachel and pulled her close. He hurriedly tossed their bags in another black SUV that had been waiting for them at Midway International Airport, and went to extricate Rachel from Jax's grasp.

Jones and Carrie were already in the front seats of the SUV and the engine was running. It was just shy of four in the morning and their window of opportunity was shrinking with every minute.

"Unhand my woman," Shane said.

"Don't be jealous, Shane," Rachel said. "I would hug anyone who got us out of that soup can on wheels. I've never been so happy to have my feet on the ground. There was a moment back there when you were looking pretty worried."

Jax sputtered and said, "Soup can on wheels?

Darlene is in her prime. She's never failed a mission."

Shane laughed and gave Jax a smug smile. "Let's go, sugar," he said, pulling Rachel to the waiting SUV.

"But what about Jax?" she asked. "Shouldn't he be coming with us?"

"Should I be worried about this odd fascination you have with him?" Shane asked.

"Well, he did just save my life," she said. "Yours too. But there's no need to be jealous. He seems like a handful, and I've already got both my hands full with you."

Shane rolled his eyes. "Jax will follow behind and grab Cutter so they can pick up your father's attorney from protective custody."

They headed east out of Midway and into the residential area of Chicago. The lights from the city could be seen in the distance, but these neighborhoods were all hidden in shadow. What few streetlights there were had been broken out, and shards of glass littered the streets along with trash and the occasional homeless person buried under newspaper piles. All of the houses were attached to each other and were no wider than one room across. The sidewalks were cracked and the trees were empty of leaves. Nothing could hide the stark depression of the street or the desperation behind the crumbling brick of the houses.

They stopped in front of the last house on the block, and Jones pulled into a cracked driveway that had weeds growing between the broken concrete. The rain had lessened to a miserable drizzle, and the headlights from the SUV caught a glimpse of the whites of someone's eyes as they lighted the alleyway. Carrie already had her gun in her lap, and Shane grabbed the .9mm out of the small of his back.

"Nice neighborhood," Rachel commented.

"We figured it was the least we could do for Mr. Norman since he was so accommodating," Jones said. "You kids stay in the car, and Carrie and I will retrieve Mr. Norman. My best advice is to just shoot anything that moves or they'll have this car stripped before we make it back outside."

Jones and Carrie left the SUV with their weapons drawn and in plain sight of anyone lurking in the area. The silence was deafening inside the car, and Rachel was sure she saw movement just outside her window, though she couldn't be sure. There were a few people who dashed back and forth from the alley to the other houses on the block, but Rachel could never get a clear glimpse of them. They were like rats scurrying from place to place, scavenging whatever they could find.

It was less than five minutes before Rachel saw the outline of Jones backlit at the front door of the row house. He held a small man by the arm and

Jones yanked him down the steps and into the rain. By the way the man was struggling, it didn't look like he was too happy to see Jones again. Carrie followed closely behind them with her weapon out and her eyes constantly moving as she looked for danger.

The back door of the SUV opened next to Rachel and the small man was unceremoniously tossed in next to her like a sack of potatoes. The man reminded her of a small wet cat. Rachel scooted closer to Shane. Jones and Carrie got back in the front seat, and they were back on the road in no time.

"I tell you, I'm going to be filing a complaint with your superior, young man," the nasally voice from beside her said.

Rachel saw Wildcat's hands tighten on the steering wheel, but he kept his eyes on the road ahead. He turned onto the highway and almost immediately the neighborhoods improved. They were now headed into the heart of the city.

"I've never been treated so poorly in my entire life," the man said, turning his gaze on Rachel. He was small of stature and his sandy hair was thinning on top. Thick glasses perched at the end of his nose and his fingernails were buffed and manicured. Despite his damp and wilted appearance, the quality of his suit was very expensive, as was the gold watch at his wrist.

"I was snatched from my home in the middle of the night, and they wouldn't even give me the courtesy of packing a bag first. For two days I've had to wear these clothes. It's just shameful. And then, as if that weren't bad enough, they blindfolded me and took me to this godforsaken place. I haven't slept a wink in fear the rats would eat me alive. And then those barbarians showed up and watched every move I made. I couldn't even use the facilities in private. It's just been a dreadful experience."

Rachel nodded sympathetically and let him wind down. The man was close to hyperventilation and was obviously prone to hysterics. She scooted closer to Shane, though she was practically sitting on his lap as it was.

"Oh dear, I haven't introduced myself. This situation has just taken its toll on my nerves. I'll have to have two sessions next week with my therapist. I'm Neville Norman, by the way," he said, extending his hand. "Third generation president and owner of Suretrust Bank."

He didn't give Rachel the opportunity to introduce herself. "And you must be Rachel Valentine. I've seen your picture on the news, so that's how I recognized you. Though you're not quite what I expected now that I'm seeing you in person for the first time. I thought you'd have a little more...class," he said, looking at her sweatshirt and jeans with disapproval. "Did you know you're wanted by the police for murder?"

Rachel was speechless. Was this guy for real?

"But of course you know," he said, shaking his head. "You're with the police right now. And it seems you have your father's talent for buying your way out of sticky situations since you're not being hauled away in handcuffs."

Rachel narrowed her eyes and felt Shane put a restraining hand on her shoulder. Mr. Norman must have seen her disgusted look because he backpedaled fast.

"Don't get me wrong, my dear. I'm so pleased you chose my bank for your nefarious purposes. According to my bank manager, people are opening new accounts left and right because of the notoriety. I'm afraid someone on my staff might have told the media you're a customer, and I do give my apologies for that, my dear, and promise to reprimand the guilty party right away. But business has really picked up. And with the economy the way it is too," he said, shaking his head.

"Glad I could be of help," Rachel said stiffly.

"And now it's my turn to help you," Mr. Norman said. "And maybe you'll think about transferring all of your father's assets over to Suretrust once he's declared legally dead."

Before Rachel could say anything to the

disgusting little man, Carrie turned around in her seat and leveled her gun right between his eyes. "Mr. Norman," she said sweetly. "Kindly shut up."

Carrie waited until she saw his nod of agreement before turning back around in her seat. Rachel saw the grin on Wildcat's face and had to duck her head down so her own smile couldn't be seen. Shane was looking out the window of the SUV, but she could feel his body shaking with laughter.

The rest of the trip was made in silence.

Suretrust Bank was directly across the street from Loyola University. It was one of the reasons Rachel had originally chosen it. When she'd first opened her account she'd been a student at the university and it had seemed the most convenient place to do her business.

Contrary to what others thought, she hadn't lived on the money her father continuously deposited into her account. She'd had a job all the way through college to supplement the athletic scholarship she'd received for target shooting, and she'd made meager deposits every week for four years. If only she'd known about Neville Norman's tendencies for high drama and his big mouth back then, she would have gladly made the trek across the city to a different bank every week.

Mr. Norman was given permission to speak again once the bank came into view. He led them around the back of the building to the employee parking lot, and Jones parked the SUV so it blocked the back entrance.

The bank was housed in what used to be an old Catholic church built sometime in the mid-1850's. The architecture was gothic, similar to most of the churches built during that time in Chicago, and they hadn't changed the outside much when it had been converted into a bank during the early part of the twentieth century. They'd replaced the stained glass windows on the street level with sturdier material and had them wired with alarms, but the stained glass on the upper floors where all the offices were held was as it always had been.

"I hope you all understand how inconvenient this is for me and my bank," Mr. Norman said. "We would have gotten national news coverage if you'd brought Ms. Valentine in to collect her things during peak traffic hours."

"We're sorry for the inconvenience," Jones said as diplomatically as possible. "But perhaps it would be best if you opened the doors and let us in before any of Angelo Valentine's men decide to use us for target practice."

Mr. Norman paled at that bit of news and

hurried to the back door. Carrie and Shane kept Rachel between them, and she didn't like the fact that they were risking their own lives trying to protect hers.

Mr. Norman opened the outer door with a key and moved into a short entryway that was barred with an electronic gate. He punched in a long series of numbers on a keypad and held his thumb to a scanner. The bars around them lifted from the ground and into the ceiling.

"No lights," Jones ordered as Mr. Norman was about to hit the main switch. "We draw as little attention as possible to ourselves."

An urgency she couldn't explain started to hammer away at Rachel's insides, and she looked behind her nervously, afraid Angelo's men were hiding around the corner. Something didn't feel right, and from the way the others held on to their weapons and swept slowly throughout the building, she thought they might be having the same feelings.

"Rachel, which direction is your safety-deposit box?" Shane asked.

"I can answer that," Mr. Norman said as if he were the star pupil in a classroom. Using his keys to unlock a drawer behind the main counter, he pulled out a large key ring that held dozens of numbered silver keys. "Ms. Valentine purchased the VIP safety-deposit box, which is housed in the basement level of the building. And as with all our VIP customers, only the best security will do," he said proudly.

Rachel rolled her eyes, perfectly aware of what kind of safety-deposit box she had and where it was located in the building, but she let Mr. Norman prattle on because despite his irritating personality, she could sense the layer of tension he was hiding behind the professional façade.

"We'll have to take the stairs down," Mr. Norman said apologetically. "We felt adding elevators would be compromising the integrity of the structure."

The stair railings were dark and polished to a high gleam, and the stairs themselves were gray-veined white marble. Rachel followed behind Mr. Norman down the stairs to the basement level. There were ornate sconces lining each side of the walls on the way down, and they cast only a small yellow glow in the darkness.

"I'm assuming I can turn the lights on down here," Mr. Norman said insolently to Jones.

"By all means," Jones said.

Mr. Norman flipped on several switches beside a round steel door and harsh fluorescent lighting came on overhead. He typed in yet another key code for the door and used his keys before turning the handle. The room wasn't terribly large. Rachel guessed an independent bank only had a handful of what they considered VIP customers. The walls were lined with numbered silver boxes and there were heavy stainless-steel tables in rows down the middle of the room. The sterility of the room didn't match the rest of the bank at all.

"Now, Ms. Valentine," Mr. Norman said. "All you need to do is use your key and collect your belongings. I can have everyone wait outside and give you some privacy if it makes you more comfortable."

"But I don't have my key," Rachel said. "It was in my apartment when it caught fire. I didn't have time to get it."

Mr. Norman clucked his tongue and shook his head. "Then I'm afraid I'll need two valid forms of ID before I can open it for you. We'll need to go back upstairs and fill out the proper paperwork. You do have ID, don't you?"

"Not on me," Rachel said with a hesitant smile.

"Open the door, Mr. Norman," Shane said.

"But it's against bank policy. If I do it for you and the word gets out, others will expect me to do the same. Or worse, they'll worry about the safety of their deposits and go elsewhere. I'm sorry, but it just can't be done. She'll have to come back when she has proper identification or the key. It's the best I can do."

Shane moved as fast as lightning, grabbing Mr. Norman by the shirt collar and holding him off the ground. Mr. Norman's face was turning purple, but Shane showed no signs of distress. "Open her box now, Mr. Norman, or I'm going to throw you through that wall over there. Nod if you understand me."

Mr. Norman nodded and Shane dropped him to the floor in a heap. He scrambled off the ground and looked through the numbered keys with shaking hands. Rachel took the wad of keys from him and walked to the far corner of the room where her box was located. Mr. Norman managed to get up off the ground with minimal fuss. He flitted around nervously, wringing his hands, either concerned the bank propriety police were going to come through the door and arrest him or Shane was going to break every bone in his body. From the way he was eyeing Shane, she had a feeling it was the latter.

"I want to press charges against this...this brute," Mr. Norman said to Jones. "You were a witness to the way he treated me. You're an FBI agent, sworn to uphold the law."

"I don't know what you're talking about," Jones said. "I didn't see anything of the kind."

"We don't have time for this," Shane said, turning his back on Mr. Norman, but Mr. Norman grabbed his sleeve and wouldn't let him leave.

"Arrest him," Mr. Norman said, voice shrill. "I demand it." The three men were gathered in the corner, Shane's face growing dark with rage and Jones trying to contain his laughter as Mr. Norman listed each of Shane's transgressions.

Rachel ignored the argument going on behind her and focused on the lockbox. It took her two tries to get the key into the lock. The nervous tension had only increased the longer they were in the bank. There were too many possibilities. Too many things that could go wrong once she had the papers in her hands. When the lock snicked open, relief consumed her. It was almost the end now. She feared her life would never be "normal" again, but if the FBI did their jobs and shut down the dangerous players on the list, maybe she could begin to live day-to-day without looking over her shoulder. Rachel pulled the rectangular silver box out of the wall and placed it on one of the heavy tables.

"Do you have it?" Carrie asked from the doorway.

The envelope with her name and address on it was exactly where she'd left it eight months before. Rachel grabbed it and shoved the box back into the wall. She just wanted to get out, and get out fast.

Rachel went to stand by Carrie in hopes the men would quit arguing and notice she'd done what she came to do.

"We need to get out of here," she said to Carrie.

"I'm not having good feelings about being here. Do you think you can get their attention?"

"I think that can be arranged," Carrie said.

Before Rachel could blink, Carrie had an arm wrapped around her throat, cutting off her air. The discharge of Carrie's gun was deafening in the small room, and Rachel watched in horror as Mr. Norman fell to the floor. Blood pooled beneath his head and ran so dark it was almost black.

"Carrie," Jones said, his weapon out automatically at the sound of gunfire. "What have you done?" The devastation and realization on his face was almost unbearable to look at.

"Don't pretend like I didn't just do you a favor," she said. Carrie positioned Rachel in front of her so the men didn't have a clear shot of her body. "I've wanted to shoot him since the first time I met him."

"I don't understand," Jones said, trying to make sense of the betrayal. "Your career. Everything you've worked for. They'll send you to prison. What about us?"

Rachel's heart went out to Jones. He was confused and hurt, but his training wouldn't let him lower his weapon. Rachel wondered if it came down to it, if Jones would be able to pull the trigger.

"Well, here's the thing, Jones," Carrie said. "There never really was an us."

A second shot sounded near Rachel's ear and

she saw the bloom of red on the front of Wildcat's shirt and the look of surprise on his face as he dropped to his knees. His weapon skidded away from his body, and he touched the wound in his chest before falling over. Rachel's ears rung and she thought she screamed out, but she couldn't be sure.

"Men are so sensitive when they're the ones who are being dumped," Carrie said in her ear. "It's pathetic."

Rachel struggled against the vise of Carrie's arms but her grip was too strong, and Rachel whimpered when Carrie pulled hard on her hair to get her to cooperate.

Mr. Norman's eyes were open and staring and she could only see the smallest movements of Wildcat's chest as he struggled to breathe. Rachel prayed the same fate didn't befall Shane. She kept her eyes locked on Shane's face, mentally telling him how much she loved him, but Shane was focused on Carrie. Shane's gaze didn't waver even as his friend lay bleeding at his feet. His .9mm was pointed at Carrie and his hand was steady.

"Carrie, this isn't the way," Shane said. "I won't hesitate to pull the trigger like Jones. I shoot to kill. Let Rachel go."

"You know I'm not going to do that, lover boy," Carrie said. "I'm making a lot of money on this deal, and I always deliver exactly what the client wants."

Her voice was different, Rachel thought. Rougher and less refined than the woman she'd thought she'd known. Hell, they'd never really known her at all. Only a few days. But Wildcat had been fooled for much longer. It took a true psychopath to live a double life of treachery and feel no remorse for the people destroyed along the way.

"You killed the other FBI agents working the Valentine case," Shane said.

Carrie shrugged and tightened her grip around Rachel's throat. "Just Agent Culver," she said. "Angelo hired me to bring him Dom, and Culver was in the way. Culver was a casualty of war, but I can't claim responsibility for the other agents. I was just the inside source for information. Angelo's men took care of the rest."

"You know Angelo isn't going to let you live once you've done what he hired you to do. That's the way Angelo works. You're smart enough to know that, Carrie."

"Angelo Valentine is a fool and his men know it," she said. "It wasn't hard to buy a few of them for extra insurance. Now I've got Rachel and the list, and as soon as I hand her over and the money is transferred my job is done. I've been Angelo's inside source for more than two years. Do you think I'm completely stupid? I've got a few tricks up my sleeve that Angelo will never see coming."

Carrie backed out of the room so she and Rachel stood at the base of the stairs.

"I'm not letting you leave here with Rachel, Carrie," Shane said. He started to move forward slowly so he could keep them both in sight.

"Stop right there," Carrie yelled, her voice breaking. The pressure was starting to get to her and her grip became so smothering that Rachel saw spots in front of her eyes. Carrie moved the gun so it was pointed at Rachel.

"You don't have a choice in the matter," Carrie said, calmer now. "Put your gun down before I shoot your girlfriend in the thigh. You can hope she doesn't bleed to death before I hand her over to Angelo. It doesn't matter one way or the other to me at this point."

Shane had lived his life by playing the odds, and he knew if he lowered his weapon then she'd put a bullet into his heart. And he'd be no good to Rachel dead. He kept his gun pointed at Carrie's head and hoped for a clear shot, but luck wasn't on his side. "That's not going to happen," he said, hoping he'd made the right choice.

"You like to live dangerously," Carrie said. "I guess she doesn't mean as much to you as I'd thought."

Shane didn't look at Rachel, afraid of what he might see in her expression. He was playing a game with a madwoman, and any distraction or break in his focus would get them all killed. Shane prayed Rachel could forgive him when it was all over.

"You lose, Shane," Carrie taunted. "I know every trick in the book, and you can't bluff your way out of this one." Carrie backed them up the stairs, and Rachel tried to slow her down as much as possible by becoming dead weight in her arms. "Enough!" Carrie said, pressing the gun hard enough to Rachel's thigh to leave a bruise. "I'll do it. I swear. If I hit an artery you'll be dead in a matter of minutes."

"Do as she says, Rachel," Shane called out. Rachel immediately stopped her struggles and went with Carrie higher up the stairs.

"Say goodbye to your lover," Carrie whispered in her ear.

"No!" Rachel screamed, fear gripping her like it never had before at the thought that Shane's life could be over in a matter of moments. She forgot about the threat of being shot and struggled frantically to try to dislodge Carrie's grip on her. Carrie took her gun and slammed it across the side of Rachel's face. Her cheek throbbed and the coppery tang of blood filled her mouth so rapidly she was choking on it. She was momentarily stunned by the blow and went limp in Carrie's arms.

"It was nice knowing you," Carrie said to Shane as she pulled something small and round out of her jacket pocket and threw it into the open door of the safety-deposit box room.

Rachel didn't even have the strength to scream as Carrie pushed her the rest of the way up the stairs and all hell broke loose behind her.

Shane saw the tiny black object that Carrie threw into the room and only had a moment to react. He kicked the metal table in front of him to its side and ducked behind it, throwing his body over Wildcat's to protect both of them as much as possible. There was nothing he could do to save Mr. Norman, but there was still life left in Wildcat, no matter how little it was.

The explosion rocketed through the entire room and pieces of metal and concrete flew from every direction. His ears rang from the force of the blast and his body shook from the vibrations. Shane shielded the back of his neck with his hands and hunkered over Wildcat, protecting his friend as best he could while the metal table they were hiding behind buckled and folded around them.

The heat was unimaginable, as the metal and concrete in the room made it feel as if they were trapped in an oven. Shane's mind was racing and he knew he had to stay in control to find Rachel alive. But the first order of business was making sure *he* stayed alive.

The smoke was thick in the room and it was almost impossible to see, but the debris finally stopped falling. Shane pushed at the heavy pieces of metal and concrete that covered his back and felt the sting of the raw scrapes over his body. The wound in his shoulder had reopened and his arm was slicked with blood, but time was of the essence and the adrenaline coursing through his body masked the pain.

He needed to get Jones out and get him help. It was obvious Jones's lung had been pierced by the bubbling pink foam around the wound.

"Come on, buddy, don't give up on me now," Shane said. The muscle Jones had added over the past couple of years added extra weight to his body, and Shane struggled to lift him into his arms. He picked his way over the debris carefully, trying not to jar his friend too much. By the time Shane reached the top of the stairs, sweat dampened his brow and the scrapes on his back and the wound in his shoulder were screaming with pain.

The cold night air and rain felt like heaven against Shane's tortured body when he finally made it out the back door of the bank. He laid Jones gently on the pavement and wondered how long it would be until emergency vehicles began to arrive. His friend was fading fast, the wheeze coming from his chest more prominent and the blue tinge around his lips growing darker in hue.

Shane was relieved to see that the SUV they'd arrived in was still in the parking lot, which meant that Carrie had someone waiting for her with another source of transportation. Probably one of Angelo's men. He opened the door of the SUV and rummaged around inside until he found what he was looking for. A Snickers bar sat in the glove compartment. Shane carefully removed the thin plastic wrapping and opened it so it was completely flat. He tossed away the chocolate and grabbed the wrapper and the phone Jones had plugged into the cigarette lighter.

He ran back to his friend and stripped off the sweatshirt he was wearing, placing it under Wildcat's head. Wildcat's eyes were open and dilated and his breathing was shallow and raspy. Shane tore his friend's shirt down the middle and exposed the tiny wound in his chest. He placed the candy wrapper over the hole and held it in place. The wheeze of air stopped leaking from Wildcat's lung and his breathing eased.

"Dammit, I don't have anything to hold this in place," Shane said. His hands were slicked with blood and he looked around for anything that he could tie around Wildcat's chest to keep the candy wrapper in place and pressure on the wound.

"In the back of the truck," Wildcat gasped out.

"Don't talk," Shane ordered. He placed Wildcat's hand against the wound and noticed the thready pulse in his wrist. "Leave your hand here, and press as hard as you can. I'll be right back."

Shane went to the back of the SUV and rummaged around until he found a black windbreaker that would fit around Wildcat's chest. Or at least he hoped it would. Shane ran back to his friend and propped him up so Wildcat was resting against Shane's knees.

"Here we go," Shane said, tying the sleeves of the jacket tightly over the wound. It would buy them a little time, but not much if emergency help didn't arrive soon. "Help is on the way," he assured Jones. "Just hold on."

Shane scrolled through the numbers on the phone he'd found in the SUV until he located the one he was looking for. He waited impatiently for someone to pick up on the other line, and when the voice answered he didn't waste time on small talk.

"This is Jax."

"Wildcat's been shot, and it's critical," Shane said. "He's got a punctured lung. Carrie is Angelo's insider, and she's taking Rachel to Angelo as we speak. Get in touch with Merlin and Dixon and make sure they don't lose sight of Angelo. He'll want to finish things tonight and clean up any loose ends." Shane heard the sirens in the distance and noticed Jones was struggling to stay conscious.

"Call me back at this number with a rendezvous point."

Shane hung up the phone and felt the pulse at Wildcat's neck. His heart was working overtime, pumping blood faster and faster even as his pulse grew weaker. Wildcat's eyes were dilated, and Shane thought he was probably going into shock.

"Hold on, Wildcat, you're not a quitter. I thought bullets couldn't touch you."

The ghost of a smile played around his friend's mouth. The sirens drew closer. "Get out of here," Jones said weakly. Blood tinged his lips as he talked and Shane fought to keep down the surge of panic.

"I'm not leaving you," Shane said. "We all leave together. That's the rule."

"I'm your commanding officer," Jones said, coughing. "Get out of here so you can save her. They'll be here soon to take care of me, but they'll arrest you if you stay. There's nothing more you can do. I've been closer to death than this before. I'll be okay."

Shane clenched his hands into fists and wished for something to punch, something hard that would hurt and take some of the pain he was feeling away. It went against every amount of training he'd ever had to leave Wildcat wounded and possibly dying in the rain.

"That's an order, Marine," Wildcat said with a last burst of strength.

Shane got up from the ground and pivoted sharply on the ball of his foot. His ears were buzzing and tears stung his eyes. He got into the SUV and pulled out of the parking lot, never looking back.

Shane drove around the outskirts of Chicago for no more than half an hour before the cell phone jingled in his pocket and Jax told him the rendezvous point was the same place they'd picked up Mr. Norman. Merlin and Dixon were waiting with information, so he turned the SUV south. Shane wasn't looking forward to going back to the neighborhood, but they didn't have a lot of options since it was best if none of them were seen involving themselves in FBI business, especially since Wildcat was no longer in the picture. Shane wasn't sure what his buddies had been up to the last couple of years, but if they'd all turned civilian like he had then they were putting themselves in a lot of risk.

Shane didn't bother with the driveway once he found his way back to the dilapidated row house. He pulled the SUV across the lawn and parked right in front of the door. A Hummer and a pickup truck were already occupying space in the driveway, and he hoped one of the vehicles would still be intact when they were ready to leave.

The front door of the house opened before he was out of the truck, and Jax stood in the doorway. No words were spoken as Shane made his way into the house. Lives were at stake and there was no time for the celebration they'd normally share at getting to work together on a job once again.

Everyone was gathered in the kitchen area, if it could even be called that, and they were already dressed for the party in black fatigues. Dixon's tall, lanky body sat erect in a straight-backed chair and he worked a toothpick nervously back and forth between his teeth. His dark blond hair was combed back from his face and tortoiseshell glasses covered his somber gray eyes. A thin black laptop sat open on the table in front of him.

Merlin sat in the chair opposite Dixon with a roll of what looked like blueprints in his hands. He was Dixon's complete antithesis—dark skinned and stocky in build, skimming just under six feet, and his black hair was unruly and rumpled like he'd just gotten out of bed. A thin scar slashed just above his right eyebrow, giving him a dangerous look that he more than deserved.

Cutter stood with his back to the wall and his arms crossed over his chest. He was almost as broad across the shoulders as Wildcat, but he didn't have the height. His hair was the color of burnished mahogany and he'd grown a short beard since the last time Shane had seen him. His coloring betrayed his Irish roots, and direct green eyes took in everything at once.

Jax stood at his back while Shane took the last available chair. Jax was the cleanup guy—the man you wanted at your back if you wanted to come out alive. He'd gotten the scar that ran from the top of his ear to the base of his cheek—ruining the pretty-boy persona he'd lived with his entire life—by watching their backs in a night raid in Iraq. They would all be dead if Jax hadn't made the sacrifice.

"Were you able to pinpoint a location for where Angelo has Rachel hidden?" Shane asked.

Merlin unrolled the blueprints onto the table. "Angelo and several of his men left his house just minutes after Jax called us and told us what had happened. They took two separate cars from the Valentine estate down Michigan Avenue to a high-rise office building that is currently under construction. Our boy Dixon did a little digging and found that the building is owned by VCorp, which is one of the companies Valentine owns to make things seem more legitimate when it comes to tax time."

"Did you see Rachel in the building?" Shane asked.

"Negative," Merlin said. "There are more than twenty floors in the building. We can only assume that's where he's keeping her as he's got men posted at all the exits, and he didn't look like he was in any hurry to leave the building."

Shane looked at the blueprints and wondered how they were ever going to find her before it was too late. It was worse than searching for a needle in a haystack. "Are any of the floors occupied?" he asked. "And can we get a visual inside from anywhere in the area?" Shane directed the question at Dixon since he was the one who could use his computer skills to break into any database in the world. The talent had come in handy more than once, and Shane was counting on it to help them this time.

Dixon's slow southern drawl often misled people about his intelligence, which according to Dixon, always gave him the upper hand. "Well, tax records show that several businesses occupy the spaces between floors twelve and eighteen." Dixon opened his computer and hit a few buttons so a screen of names and numbers showed up. "But a closer look at these companies show they don't really exist at all. I hacked into a few of the past surveillance tapes and there's never anyone shown going in or out of the building. It's just a dummy operation as far as I can see."

He hit another series of commands and the blueprints came up on screen. "I've blacked out the floors where the offices are located. My gut says he wouldn't use those to hold anyone hostage. It would be inconvenient if the IRS showed up on his doorstep and wanted to take a look around."

Shane could read between the lines. What Dixon really meant was that Angelo wouldn't want to take the chance of dirtying the furnished areas with anything like blood. Shane put the thought out of his mind that even as he was sitting here trying to find a way to save Rachel, she could already be past the point of saving.

"Floors one through twelve are in the skeleton phase of renovations," Dixon continued. "But I'd bet my money that he's got her stashed either on nineteen or twenty. Renovations are a little further along on the upper floors. From what I can tell he's turning them into apartments of sorts."

"Can we get access?" Shane asked.

"Well, that's going to be a little trickier seeing as how there's just the five of us against at least twelve men that we saw guarding the building. Maybe more. The Hancock Hotel is directly across the street from the building, and it should give you a good view of those top two floors from the roof level. You can set up over there and the rest of us will go in on foot and take out as many as we can to give you plenty of time and the best shot possible."

Shane broke out in a cold sweat at the thought of what he was going to have to do. Hadn't he been in almost the exact same situation two years ago? And failed miserably? Now the woman he loved, because there was no doubt what he felt for Rachel, was putting all her trust and her life in his hands. God, he hoped the saying was wrong about history repeating itself.

"Are you okay, Ace?" Cutter asked.

"Yeah," Shane said, standing. "Let's move out. We've only got a couple of hours until daylight."

Chapter Fifteen

Icy cold water hit Rachel in the face and brought her gasping to consciousness. She didn't remember the drive to wherever she was now or how long she'd been unconscious. She only remembered the fiery explosion in the basement of the bank and that Shane was buried somewhere in the rubble.

She'd screamed and fought against Carrie, not caring about her own safety, and she'd tried to run back down the stairs and into chaos. She remembered Carrie's arms struggling to hold her and that someone else had been there. That's when the second blow had come and it had felt like the back of her skull had exploded. It was lights out after that.

Her vision was blurred and the icy water wracked her body with chills. Her thoughts were scattered and her mind wouldn't cooperate as she tried to piece things together. The right side of her face ached with every laborious breath she took and her eye was swollen almost completely shut. The fierce headache throbbing through her skull was from the blow to the back of the head she'd received. She tried to take stock of the rest of her body, but she couldn't assess the damage since her ankles were tied to a chair with sturdy rope and her hands were cuffed behind her.

"Rise and shine, sleeping beauty," Carrie's voice sang out. "We wouldn't want your uncle to make the trip all this way only to find you'd passed out. Torture is more fun when the victim is awake. I'm sure you understand that."

Rachel's wet hair hung down in front of her face and she didn't have the strength to raise her head and give Carrie the glare she deserved. Her vision swam and she had to focus to stay conscious.

"I hope he kills you," Rachel rasped. Her throat was dry and the words protested as she tried to force them out. "I'll be glad to watch you die, but I promise you if he doesn't that I will hunt you down and do it myself."

"Ooh, that's scary," Carrie said. Her casual laugh chilled Rachel's blood. "Are you going to come back as a ghost and haunt me?"

Rachel gritted her teeth and forced her head up

so she could look Carrie in the eyes, ignoring the pain that was radiating from her skull. Carrie was still dressed in FBI black and her weapon was holstered at her side. But it was her face that gave Rachel the chills. How could anyone be that good of an actress when the insanity was so transparent behind the eyes? Blood was smeared on her cheek and her blond hair was matted and mussed from the aftershocks of the explosion.

"You won't get away with what you did to Shane. To Jones. You're a sick woman. Beyond anyone's help. Which means hell is too good for you. So I'll do whatever I have to do," Rachel swore. "As long as it means you're dead."

Carrie's smile froze in place at the look Rachel gave her. Both women were determined not to back down, but there was fear inside Carrie that hadn't been there a moment ago. An elevator pinged in the distance and footsteps echoed on the concrete floors. Rachel took a moment to look at her surroundings and try to figure out where she was.

She was surrounded by windows. And from the view she knew she was fairly high up. The lights from the hotels and other businesses shone through the windows and lit the floor she was occupying. Stacks of lumber and buckets of paint were scattered around the room, and the metal folding chair she sat in seemed to be the only furniture.

The sight of her Uncle Angelo walking into the room was her worst nightmare come to life. He looked so much like her father it brought a pang to her heart, but looks was where the similarities ended. Angelo had a brutality to him that her father had never possessed. Even with the position of power over the mob Dom had obtained over the years, he'd never resorted to cruelty to get what he wanted. And for a time the other mob families had respected that and followed the same guidelines he'd set.

Angelo clucked his tongue at the sight of her. "Well, niece, I've certainly seen you looking better. The swelling on your face might make it harder for the authorities to identify your body. But don't worry. I'm sure they'll figure it out sooner or later. The FBI has ways of finding such things out. Isn't that right, Agent Layne?" he asked Carrie.

Rachel could only handle one threat at a time so didn't bother looking at her Uncle Angelo. She stared at Carrie. If she was going to die, she wanted the other woman to know she'd meant every word she'd said about her fate.

Carrie was doing everything possible to ignore Rachel. There were undercurrents in the room that Rachel didn't understand. Carrie was watching the two men who stood at Angelo's back and trying to relay some unspoken communication to them. They looked like exactly what they were.

Hired thugs. Their suits were boxy and their minds empty except for whatever orders were tossed their way, and Carrie's frustration was growing palpable.

Angelo didn't like being ignored. "Now, tell me, niece, who did this to your pretty face?"

Rachel didn't answer. She just kept her glare on Carrie.

"Ahh," Angelo said. "I believe I can connect the dots." He turned around and faced Carrie, and she stood defiantly in front of him.

"Has the money been transferred?" she asked.

"Yes. And I even added the extra hundred thousand you demanded to bring me Rachel alive. Though it wasn't in good form to mark her like this. She won't last nearly as long now."

"I did what I had to do," she said shrugging. She pulled out the envelope from the inside of her jacket and handed it over to Angelo. "And here's the list as requested. For no extra charge."

Angelo pulled out the list and scanned it before folding it and putting it in the inside pocket of his suit jacket. "I assume your travelling companions have been taken care of as well?"

"Yes. You could say they had an unfortunate accident," Carrie said, smirking in Rachel's direction. "Now, if you'll give me a minute to call and make sure the funds have been transferred into my account, I'll be on my way. Not that I don't believe you about the money. But I make it a point to never trust anyone."

Carrie walked over to the two guards as if she were going to tell them something, but the words never made it out of her mouth. Angelo moved with a speed not many people knew him capable of. The buck knife he habitually carried in a sheath at the small of his back was in his hand in a matter of seconds, and the lights from the hotel across the street flashed across the six-inch silver blade.

Angelo grabbed Carrie by the hair and held the knife to her throat. Her hand automatically went to the holster at her side, but Angelo pressed harder with the blade until Rachel could see the thin line of blood dripping from the tip of the knife. Carrie dropped her hands.

"Do something, you fools," she called out to the two guards. "Kill him."

The men stood still and looked straight ahead, ignoring her pleas.

"Did you really think I wouldn't know about you bribing my men to turn against me?" Angelo asked. "You thought you were so clever, didn't you? Didn't you?" he demanded.

"Y-y-yes," Carrie stuttered.

"You know nothing of inspiring loyalty. Money is not the only motivator a person has. Do you think those men are more afraid of you than they are of me?" he whispered, running the blade of the knife down the side of her cheek.

Carrie's eyes were wide with fear and with the knowledge she'd gone too far.

"P-p-please," she begged. "I didn't mean it."

"I'd enjoy torturing you, but I just can't waste the time," Angelo said. He jerked back hard on her hair and sliced the knife across her throat. A spray of blood arced through the air and Angelo stepped back to avoid the sticky substance from getting on his clothes. He let Carrie fall to the ground and stepped over her body. He held the knife up in front of Rachel—the knife still coated with the blood of a woman she'd promised would die.

Rachel felt no sorrow in the death of Carrie. But she felt fear as her own death stared her in the face.

There was a pool on the roof of the Hancock Hotel. The way it glowed an eerie bluish green would be one of the things that would stay in his mind forever.

Shane didn't have a problem gaining access to the roof in the middle of the night. It had actually been rather simple. He'd showered the dust and blood from his face and body and changed into clothes that Cutter had tossed his way. And they'd brought his rifle. It was concealed inside a black suitcase.

He'd checked into the hotel using Cutter's identification, since they looked the most alike physically. Not to mention checking in under Shane's own name would get him arrested as soon as they entered his information into the computer. He paid cash for the room and requested one of the upper floors. The bored desk clerk barely gave him a second glance as he signed Cutter's name to the receipt and she handed him the key card.

Shane rode the elevator up to seventeen. When the doors opened, he got off on his floor but walked past his room to the stairs at the end of the long hallway. He climbed the remaining three stories up and used his key card to access the roof level.

The wind and rain was frigid and pelted his face when he opened the door. The door shut behind him, and he took the cell phone Dixon had given him out of his pocket. Dixon had the phone rigged so that one swipe across the electronic key slot would make the door unusable to anyone else. He'd have the whole rooftop to himself, not that anyone else would be crazy enough to be on the roof in the miserable weather besides him.

In the hotter months of the year, swimming or relaxing on the roof with the cool breeze would probably bring much-needed relief to the body, but right now it was pure misery. The wind and other elements were always a factor when setting up for a shot, and he'd have to be careful not to overcompensate. He'd only have one chance.

Shane dropped the suitcase he was carrying onto the ground near the edge of the roof and unzipped it. He pulled a pair of night goggles over his eyes but then immediately tossed them aside. The lights from the hotel were too bright for them to do him any good. He'd have to rely on a pair of high-powered binoculars and his scope. It was still a good ways off till dawn, so he didn't have to worry about that factor.

Shane set up the tripod for his rifle with quick, easy movements. The motions were as familiar to him as putting on his clothes every morning. Maybe more. He hunkered down on the cold roof and ignored the wet seeping into his clothes. His only concern was the job at hand.

His friends were twenty stories below, waiting on his signal before they infiltrated the building. He knew the four of them would do exactly what they'd set out to and get rid of all the threats that lurked in the building, but Rachel's safety would rely solely on him.

He used the binoculars and started on the lower floors of the building across the street. Angelo's goons were scattered around the entrances on the lower levels of the building and near the elevators. These guys were lower level security at best.

None of them were very alert at this time of night. He saw a couple of them dozing in straight-back chairs or on the floor against the walls. That would just make their job that much easier.

Rachel hadn't come into his sights yet, but he hadn't expected her to. According to Dixon's research, she'd be on one of the top floors. And Dixon was never wrong. Shane moved the binoculars up floor by floor until he came to the top level. If it weren't for the binoculars he never would have been able to see inside. The glass had already been tinted dark in preparation for the apartment that was being constructed.

And what he saw inside the room sickened him. Rachel was bound to a chair and her face was swollen and bloody. He could only see her in profile, but she was looking Angelo straight in the eyes as he talked to her, never backing down. There were two men at Angelo's back, and Shane could tell by the way they stood that they were much more dangerous than the men positioned on the bottom floors. There was a body on the floor that looked like Carrie, but he couldn't be a hundred percent sure. At least Angelo had taken that task out of his hands.

Shane used the cell phone Dixon had given him to signal that he'd found Rachel, and that the rest of the team could enter the building when ready. He couldn't worry about what they were doing or if they were walking into a trap. He could only focus on Rachel and the man who wanted her dead.

Shane breathed slowly through his mouth and slowed his heartbeat before looking through the scope on his rifle and placing his finger on the trigger. Thoughts of what had happened two years ago flooded his brain with the images of horror he saw in his dreams every night, and he cursed as he pulled away from the scope and lay flat on his back on the ground.

He had to get it together. This was a completely different circumstance, and Rachel wasn't Maggie. The cold rain beat down on his face, but his body temperature was hot. His pulse jumped in his neck and his thoughts were scattered. He closed his eyes and did a few breathing exercises, and then he crawled back into position and looked through the scope once again.

From what he could see, it looked like Angelo's rage was escalating, and Shane knew he could wait no longer.

For the first time in his life Shane's finger shook as he placed it on the trigger.

"Do you know why I wanted you brought here to me?" Angelo asked Rachel.

"Because you're insane," she said. She would have smiled just to piss him off, but the movement would have hurt too much.

"You always did have a smart mouth. Your father didn't discipline you nearly enough in my opinion."

"Leave my father out of this. In your wildest dreams you'll never come close to being half the man he is."

"Don't you mean was?" Angelo asked with a Cheshire cat smile. He pulled the handkerchief out of his jacket pocket and wiped down the blade in his hand.

Rachel felt the color drain from her face and she became nauseated. She'd waited all this time and had never known the truth about what had happened to her father. She thought she'd prepared herself for the worst, but she'd sorely miscalculated.

Angelo flipped the knife in his hand and kept his eyes steady on hers. "Come now, Rachel. Don't disappoint me. Aren't you going to ask what happened to him? Aren't you the least bit curious to know how he died?"

Rachel bit the inside of her cheek to keep herself from screaming out loud. NO! she wanted to yell. She didn't want to know what had happened to her father. But the reasonable side of her brain told her she needed the closure. Needed to be able to finally lay her father to rest.

"What did you do to him?" she finally asked.

Angelo smiled at her and continued tossing his knife in the air, end over end, so Rachel was almost hypnotized by the motion.

"I paid Carrie to bring me Dom and the original list that he'd handed over to Agent Culver. She brought me Dom as I'd asked, but unfortunately the list was nowhere to be found. No one seems to know what happened to it, but I have my own theories. Carrie was a greedy young woman, and she probably thought having her own copy might come in useful at some point. I couldn't blame her really. It's exactly why I wanted the list for myself. I let the transgression slide because I still had need of her inside the FBI. It's not as easy to bribe law enforcement as it used to be, and Carrie did have her uses."

Angelo tossed his knife to the other hand, and Rachel noticed the guards at Angelo's back were beginning to get antsy. Maybe they weren't as comfortable with a sociopathic boss as they liked to think.

"I'm on the list, you know," Angelo said. "Imagine how you'd feel if your own brother was going to turn you in. I couldn't let it happen, and the other families agreed with me. Everyone was so sad to get rid of Dom."

Anger flooded Angelo's face and he continued to toss the knife, round and round, only he hadn't noticed how tight he was gripping the blade each time he caught it. Blood dripped steadily down his wrist and onto the floor. "Everyone loved Dom like he was Santa Claus. People aren't afraid of Santa Claus. He was ruining us all."

Rachel jerked against the cuffs around her wrists, but found they were cinched tight. Angelo was losing control quickly and she'd already decided she wasn't going to go down easy. She wouldn't just sit quietly and wait for him to slice her throat. It just wasn't in her nature.

"Dom was a pathetic excuse for a man. I brought him to this very building and sat him just as you are now. I didn't give him the easy way out like I did with your friend here," he said, pushing Carrie's body over with the tip of his shoe so her gaping throat was exposed. "He didn't even have the decency to take it like a man when I started to work on him. He begged and pleaded the whole time, crying like a little girl, for me to stay away from you. I, of course, would have been glad to accommodate a dying man's last wishes, but then I found out he'd sent you a little surprise in the mail. I can admit I got a little overzealous with your father. He didn't last nearly as long as I'd have liked him to. Sometimes I forget my own strength and cut a little too deep."

Angelo looked down at his hand and noticed

the blood for the first time. "See what I mean," he said, holding his palm up for her to see.

The guards at Dom's back were moving toward the elevator, each of them talking on their headsets, repeating the same command for each station to check in. Angelo didn't notice. He was in his own world.

Rachel wiggled her ankles and tried desperately to loosen the rope at her feet. She'd stopped watching the flipping knife and her gaze followed the two guards around the room. They pressed the button for the elevator, but it never arrived, so they split up and went to each side of the floor where the emergency exit stairs were located.

A hard slap brought Rachel's attention back to Angelo, bringing a moan of pain to her lips. He'd hit the same cheek as Carrie had earlier and blood dribbled down her chin. She breathed through her nose to fight the nausea and couldn't find the strength to groan when Angelo yanked her up by the hair so she was looking him in the face.

"I haven't finished my story yet," he said. "You're being very rude. Now, where was I?"

Rachel didn't make the mistake of taking her eyes off him again.

"Oh, yes. I had just killed your father. It's a moment I'll always remember. And now I have you in exactly the same spot. Ironic, isn't it?"

"What did you do with him?" Rachel was

barely able to get the question out. Her face was swollen to the point where her mouth would only open so far and talking was difficult.

"What did I do with him?" Angelo laughed. "I'm not completely heartless. He was my brother after all. I gave him a decent burial. Last spring I had the most beautiful crop of roses bloom in my gardens. I like to think it's because Dom is such good fertilizer."

Tears coursed down Rachel's cheeks and she could tell her uncle was finished grandstanding. Her end had come.

"Are you ready, Rachel?" he asked softly. "I'll try not to make it over too soon." The knife was back in his hand in the blink of an eye, but the chaos at the stairwell finally got his attention. Four men dressed in black, with their faces painted to match, burst through the doors. Rachel recognized Jax and the tears started falling faster. The fighting at the stairs was intense, and the guards put up a struggle that would have evened things up considerably if the numbers had been the same.

Angelo didn't waste time trying to save the lives of his bodyguards. He moved slowly behind Rachel and took her by the hair.

The guards were both face down on the floor and the four men in black were the only ones left standing. They each had their weapons pointed to the ground so as not to put Rachel in the line of fire.

"Congratulations, gentlemen. You've found me. But I won't be taken down alone. She'll die one way or the other."

The blade of the knife bit into her skin and she held back a whimper of pain. She closed her eyes tightly and thought of Shane—about the last night they'd spent together and the lifetime they'd never get to see.

Glass shattered from across the room and she was left with no time to react. One minute she was praying for a quick death and the next her killer lay crumpled on the ground behind her. She was frozen in shock, and the reality of what had happened didn't begin to set in until Jax came over and began to untie her.

"Oh, God," she said, choking on a sob. "Shane?" She grabbed Jax's arm as soon as her hands were free. "He's still alive?"

"Alive and well," he assured her. "But I'd give him another couple of minutes before he makes it over here. He's not as young as he used to be."

Rachel laughed through her tears. "I need to see him. Don't let anyone take me away until I see him."

"He'd kill me if I tried," Jax said. "No offense, honey, but you're not looking so good right now.

Maybe you could make your reunion a quick one so we can get you to the hospital."

"Ambulance is on its way," one of the other men called out. "Along with the FBI. Should be an entertaining couple of hours."

As soon as the bullet left his rifle, Shane knew he'd made a direct hit. He barely took the time to disassemble his rifle and put it back in the suitcase before he was running back into the hotel. He rode the twenty floors down with agonizing impatience and ignored the stares of the desk clerks as he ran through the lobby and out the doors.

Traffic was light outside and he ran across Michigan Avenue, dodging taxis and other vehicles until he stood in front of Angelo Valentine's highrise. He barely noticed the bodies that littered the floor on the inside or how smoothly the elevator ran as he rode his way to the top. All he could think about was Rachel. She was alive. And if she'd have him he'd make sure she stayed safe for the rest of his life.

The elevator doors opened and he ran onto the floor he'd just minutes before been looking at through his scope. He ignored the congratulations from his team members and searched for Rachel.

She was sitting on the floor with her back against the wall and Cutter was looking over her bruises.

Suddenly he found himself unsure what to do. How to react. But then Rachel opened her eyes and looked straight at him as if she'd sensed him there all along. She held out her hand to him and he knew exactly where he belonged.

Shane went to her and the sight of her beautiful face, so swollen and battered, made his knees weak and his trigger finger itch to kill the bastard one more time.

"Oh, baby," he said, taking her hand. He didn't know where else to touch her that wouldn't cause her pain.

"I'm okay," she said. "I thought you were dead." Fat tears gathered at the corners of her eyes and rolled down her cheeks. "I was so afraid, but when I thought I was going to die you were the only thing I could think of. And then you saved me."

"Ssh," Shane said. "Try not to talk. I know it hurts."

She nodded at him. Shane heard the stretcher being wheeled off the elevator and knew his time alone with her was short. He took a breath and prayed she'd understand what she meant to him. "It was you, Rachel, that saved me," he finally said. "I'm not whole without you, and you've managed to do something I thought was impossible."

"What's that?" she asked.

"You've chased the nightmares away. Love has that ability." He didn't move as the medics came and kneeled beside them.

"I hope you're planning to marry me soon," she said. "Because when I get out of the hospital I plan to pick up where we left off at the safe house."

He laughed and kissed her softly on the forehead. "You've got a deal, Valentine."

Epilogue

Being Shane's wife had its perks.

There was the obvious reason—passion and desire and need all rolled into the vows they'd shared. Shane hadn't wasted any time setting up her hospital room with an abundance of flowers and the hospital chaplain. She hadn't needed or wanted a big wedding. Just him. The wedding was just the starting point, not the final destination.

Her recovery time was the only thing that delayed their new life together. She'd had multiple surgeries on her jaw, but eventually the physical pain and healing had subsided and made way for the emotional healing she knew needed to happen.

She'd never known what it felt like to not be a Valentine. To not have your life dissected by those who only wanted to see you fail. And the twenty-four-hour protection Shane had arranged to have outside her hospital room was a stark reminder where she came from and that the battle wasn't over yet.

Their names had been cleared, but list was in the hands of multiple alphabet agencies, and there'd already been arrests. It had been her father who'd made the list and decided to turn his longtime friends, enemies, and competitors in to the authorities. But with Dominic Valentine out of the picture she was the next best substitute for their vengeance.

She and Shane had a choice to make—they could live the rest of their lives hidden—new identities and careers through Witness Protection. Or they could use the resources they had—the friends and contacts and favors to be called in—and they could let those who wanted her head on a platter know that what happened to her Uncle Angelo and his men was just a sampling of what would happen to them if anything happened to Rachel or anyone else she loved. She was off the table. No longer affiliated with the life that had made her family one of the most notorious in the country.

She didn't know how the men Shane had served with had gotten the message across, but they'd struck fear into the hearts of those who might want to see her harmed.

No one cared about Rachel Quincy. She was just a regular woman—happily married to the man of her dreams with a design firm in the heart of the French Quarter.

Spanish moss blew lazily in the trees as she swung in the hammock in their backyard. Spring was a time of new birth—new beginnings—and she inhaled the sweet aroma of the honeysuckle blooming along the fence.

They'd come back to New Orleans. It was Shane's home, but it had felt like home to her the moment she stepped foot in the city. It was alive with music and scents and cultures and food—always changing and growing. And tucked away in a small corner of the Garden District was their new home, majestic and romantic, not far from where her and Shane's lives had first intersected.

"I figured I'd find you out here lazing the day away," Shane said, coming through the French doors and onto the patio.

She couldn't help but smile. Despite the danger that lurked inside him, there was a gentleness that soothed her soul as he walked toward her. He'd been working. He was dressed in black BDUs and a black T-shirt. And already she felt the slow spin in her stomach of attraction. She'd never get enough of him.

"You're home early," she said. "That's a pleasant surprise."

"You too," he said. "I thought you had some big client today."

She shrugged and rolled out of the hammock, taking his hand. "I found myself unable to concentrate. I kept thinking of...other things." She kissed his bottom lip and smiled seductively as he sucked in a breath.

"You did tell me that New Orleans is a city that keeps its own hours," she continued, pulling his shirt up and exposing the muscled abdomen beneath. "There are no timetables here. It's the city that care forgot."

"*Laissez les bon temps rouler,*" Shane whispered against her mouth.

"What brings you home so early?" she asked.

He picked her up and she wrapped her legs around him. "I was thinking about this."

"*Laissez les bon temps rouler,* indeed," she said.

Acknowledgments

Getting a book to publication takes an amazing team of people. I'm fortunate to have had these people in my corner for years.

To my editor—Imogen Howson for always making me better.

To my cover designer—Dar Albert for always blowing me away with your talent.

To my children—You're all so special. You have gifts and abilities beyond measure, and I'm excited to see what God has in store for each of you.

To Scott—thank you for answering a ridiculous amount of law enforcement questions and acting out weird scenarios with me. Any mistakes are mine alone.

About the Author

Liliana Hart is a *New York Times*, *USA Today*, and Publisher's Weekly bestselling author of more than eighty titles. After starting her first novel her freshman year of college, she immediately became addicted to writing and knew she'd found what she was meant to do with her life. She has no idea why she majored in music.

Since publishing in June 2011, Liliana has sold more than ten-million books. All three of her series have made multiple appearances on the *New York Times* list.

Liliana can almost always be found at her computer writing, hauling five kids to various activities, or spending time with her husband. She calls Texas home.

If you enjoyed reading this, I would appreciate it if you would help others enjoy this book, too.

Recommend it. Please help other readers find this book by recommending it to friends, readers' groups and discussion boards.

Review it. Please tell other readers why you liked this book by reviewing.

Connect with me online:
www.lilianahart.com

facebook.com/LilianaHart
instagram.com/LilianaHart
bookbub.com/authors/liliana-hart

Also by Liliana Hart

JJ Graves Mystery Series
Dirty Little Secrets

A Dirty Shame

Dirty Rotten Scoundrel

Down and Dirty

Dirty Deeds

Dirty Laundry

Dirty Money

A Dirty Job

Dirty Devil

Playing Dirty

Dirty Martini

Dirty Dozen

Dirty Minds

Addison Holmes Mystery Series
Whiskey Rebellion

Whiskey Sour

Whiskey For Breakfast

Whiskey, You're The Devil

Whiskey on the Rocks

Whiskey Tango Foxtrot

Whiskey and Gunpowder

Whiskey Lullaby

The Scarlet Chronicles

Bouncing Betty

Hand Grenade Helen

Front Line Francis

The Harley and Davidson Mystery Series

The Farmer's Slaughter

A Tisket a Casket

I Saw Mommy Killing Santa Claus

Get Your Murder Running

Deceased and Desist

Malice in Wonderland

Tequila Mockingbird

Gone With the Sin

Grime and Punishment

Blazing Rattles

A Salt and Battery

Curl Up and Dye

First Comes Death Then Comes Marriage

Box Set 1

Box Set 2

Box Set 3

The Gravediggers

The Darkest Corner

Gone to Dust

Say No More